Sinister

For more excellent works of fiction, visit Inkandquillpress.com

Held Hostage

By Ace Rhodes

I just can't believe this is happening to me...Carl thought in frustration as he drove his car home from another, what should have been, routine day of work. I mean what could they possibly want, I don't need a security clearance to do what I do, why are they checking into me!?

Is this about the military stuff? Maybe about that settlement for my hand a few years ago...his head rocketed as he came up with scenario after scenario and possibility after possibility, but for the life of him he just couldn't connect the dots.

For nearly a month, Carl had heard the occasional whispers and off-colored comments of coworkers. He saw the way they looked at him with pity, at times even disdain or anger. Once recently, he even swore he'd seen a hooded figure in his periphery watching him from around a corner, only to dash away when he looked across the room in that direction.

But the bigger worry was the way even his wife Stella was acting around him. But surely that was just coincidence, there's no way she could be involved with any of this, right? His mind raced, a condition that was sadly and quickly becoming his norm.

In fact, the more often he thought about it, only his two boys seemed immune from the assuming, measured looks and comments he'd been receiving as of late, only they seemed to not be in on the secrets levied against him.

Tyler, age nine, and Tommy, five, were the light and life of both he and Stella's life. They were the reason Carl got up every day and trudged on, even on the days when he felt like quitting all together, even through the confusing and frustrating events of late.

But that was silly too, they were just boys and didn't count, couldn't count either, right? At first, he dismissed the thoughts surrounding them, but as the days turned to weeks and the weeks crept up close to a month, they had become the best anchor to prove his sanity to himself.

And there it was again, why...why and how and for what? What had he done? Why was this happening to him? How was seemingly everyone besides his children off-put by him, or worse angry at him?

Home finally. He walked up the sidewalk to the house and opened the back door to a tidal wave of tiny human flesh crashing into him shouting, "POP your home! Hey Pop! Pop, let's wrestle!" A small reprieve from the worry, but a reprieve, nonetheless.

After saying hello and spending some time with Stella and the boys he headed downstairs to his tool room. It was a small space he had claimed when they first moved in and it had since become a gathering place for tools, and various other objects he'd figure he'd use one day down the line.

After the first couple weeks of this phenomena, he began to document his experiences throughout the day, and in the evenings he would retreat here to this room and read over his notes to try and make sense of what was happening. It was baffling, the first few pages of the notebook were spotty, isolated incidents happening here and there, but just a few pages in the notes grew longer and ran for pages, until now, now there was just so much. His notebook was filling up quickly and tonight's addition would be a lengthy one again.

There were the now normal sour looks from Jan and Darla, the office ladies, the first two people at work he saw when he walked in most mornings. Though today they stopped talking mid conversation, and they seemed to tense up as soon as they saw it was him in the doorway. It was so silent as he walked through the front office you could hear the proverbial pin-drop, and he could certainly hear Jan pick up the phone to alert Brad the office manager that he had arrived as he rounded the corner that connected the reception and back offices.

He arrived early, mind you, as he did every day, so why would they need to call Brad. It was stuff like this in the beginning that bothered him, but as it progressed, it also seemed to be turning darker. It was only a week ago when his friend John stopped talking to him, and two days ago when John made his way over to Carl to tell him that "they were watching him" and to "be careful, buddy".

When Carl pressed him with, "Who are they?" John seemed to look drained as he replied, "..management, coworkers, probably everyone man."

"What happened, what did I do?" Carl pleaded.

John took a long sympathetic look into Carl's eyes and for a moment it seemed as if he was going to tell him right then and there, but ultimately, he shook his head and walked away.

That was the last Carl had heard from his "friend" until the day everything changed. During the time in between it was, "sorry man, I don't want to be involved," or "yeah...uh huh, yeah."

That week, Carl found himself becoming increasingly isolated. Even casual conversations with coworkers, those few he was still privy to, turned awkward. Meetings felt like inquisitions. The lunchroom, once a sanctuary of camaraderie, now echoed with hushed conversations that abruptly halted whenever he entered.

And it wasn't just at work. The situation was beginning to escalate even in his neighborhood. He'd often see cars idling outside his home at odd hours, their headlights casting eerie beams in the twilight. Neighbors he'd known for years suddenly avoided his gaze, hurrying their children indoors when he passed. And it was from here at home earlier this evening that he would focus his study tonight as he wrote with a quivering hand, "it seems to have Stella too..."

His evenings were his only solace, at least for the time being. And though Stella had begun to grow distant, her once warm smile, tonight seemed to be replaced with a vacant stare. Their conversations as of late were tough but tonight, they were peppered with ambiguous comments that felt like veiled threats. This evening just after an uncomfortable and quiet dinner she said, "Carl, maybe you need to take a break...go somewhere... find yourself." This wasn't the Stella he knew.
"What the hell do you mean go somewhere!?" He insisted, the pain in his tone showing in his voice that now his wife too seemed to be blaming him for some unknown crime. Then something wild, and truly unnatural happened that shocked and scared Carl to his core.

Stella opened her mouth, but no words came out, just a scream from somewhere inside, distant. In that instant he watched her face twist and contort into something not quite human. He winced, and as he backed away terrified and in the next instant, it was like the moment had never even happened. He was so scared he thought he might piss himself. She was normal again in an instant, in fact she looked almost as startled as he did, almost. What the fuck was happening? And although the rest of the evening was relatively uneventful and Stella asked him several times what he was talking about, he could see a difference in her, in her eyes, in her soul.

That night he lay in the boys' room on the floor, bound to protect them from whatever had attached itself to Stella. He didn't sleep at all, although he pretended to. As he lay, through squinted eyes, he could see Stella silently crack the door open only to stand deadly still and stare, her face in darkened shadow. She stood for what seemed like hours but as scared as he was he had no real concept of time, and then she retreated slowly to her room. This happened over and over until the early morning hours; He never dared move, and she never advanced more than the doorway.

Although he couldn't really make out the details of her face, he knew, he *could see enough* to know it was the twisted face he'd seen earlier that evening staring at him. He thought all through the night. If she was going to hurt the boys, he reasoned she would have tried while they all lay helpless in their sleep, no this was about him, all about him. And in some small way he felt validated, something was going on. Something he couldn't yet explain, but he now knew he wasn't making it up in his head.

He got up the next day determined to go on the offensive and figure it all out.

He began setting up recording devices around his house and at work, hoping to find evidence of anything that seemed amiss. Most nights from then on out, after the boys were asleep and Stella went to bed, Carl would sit alone in the dimly lit basement tool room, headphones on, listening to every murmur and rustle, trying to decipher their meanings. He would check on the boys several times throughout the night making sure they were okay.

He couldn't remember the last time he'd slept for more than a few minutes. Everything the last two or three days had seemed relatively normal, except for the normal work isolation, but he couldn't shake the feeling of some unknown impending dread ahead of him.

Then one evening, a few days later, as he was going through his recordings, he stumbled upon something that, again, chilled the very blood in his veins. It was one of the recorders from work. He could distinctly hear two male voices, which he recognized as his co-workers, Mark Pats and James Smitty. The conversation was fragmented, broken, but he could make out the phrases, "He knows too much," "It's only a matter of time," and "... must be eliminated."

Even worse, both voices were laced with a second deeper voice, a sound not quite human that hummed alongside his former friends', mimicking their words with its own.

The fear gnawing at him intensified. Feeling more vulnerable than ever, Carl thought of the only two people he could trust – Tyler and Tommy. Most nights they all played and talked, though he tried to keep the conversations light. The following evening however, clinging to his sanity he made a pact with Tyler. He handed him a small envelope. "Keep this safe, hide it so not even I can find it okay, buddy," he whispered, his voice choking with emotion. Inside the envelope was a lock of Carl's hair and a note detailing his experiences, as a last-resort piece of evidence should anything happen to him.

He began to recount to Tyler some, but not all the, events he'd seen and heard. He withheld the demonic stuff and about what he'd seen with his mother. He did ask Tyler and Tommy if mommy had been acting strangely to them, to which Tyler replied no and Tommy explained she hadn't made him PB&J yesterday like he'd requested.

He pulled Tyler aside and told his son that he was afraid, that he was afraid people were coming to get him. Tyler cried, but tried to put on a brave face, determined to offer what help he could to his father. It was hard seeing his father like this, especially since before this had all started his father told him he'd do anything for him.

The days following had become an agonizing blur for Carl, each more oppressive than the last. The world seemed darker, the walls closed in, as if reality itself was conspiring against him. His only reprieve was his time with the boys. And one fateful evening, it all finally came to a head.

Returning home from a particularly grueling day at work, Carl found his house unusually silent. The lively atmosphere, the children's laughter, even the sound of television- all were conspicuously absent. Panic surged through him. Rushing through the rooms, he found Stella sitting on the couch, surrounded by unfamiliar faces. Men in suits sat in a semicircle around Stella, their expressions stern.

"Carl," Stella's voice was shaky, tears streaming down her face, "I'm so sorry, I just couldn't take it anymore, I couldn't do it to the boys." Confusion muddled his thoughts as he pleaded with his wife "why?". As he backed away, he began to get dizzy. He looked around, trying to make sense of the situation, when he was suddenly grabbed by several strong grips, and then he felt a sharp prick on his arm. As his world slowed, his captures showed their true forms.

Demonic, dark, and twisted faces replaced those that he saw moments before.

His last sight was of Stella, her face twisting into the same face he witnessed weeks ago, giggling and staring at him from across the room.

When he awoke, he was in a dark room, his arms and legs restrained. A man approached him, "Carl, you need to eat your food and drink your medicine HAHAHAHAHAHA!"

The food he had gestured to was rotten, the "medicine" was foul, a viscous liquid with a sweet tinge that he was sure was poison but looked to him like bile. When he looked back to the man it was the same hideous twisted demonic face he had seen at his home.

He was terrified and exhausted, he already felt that they'd won, though he still didn't even know why he was playing their game in the first place.

In the heart of his prison, days stretched to time he couldn't measure, the weight of each passing moment stretched and felt longer and longer than the last. He remained trapped in the dimly lit room. Refusing to eat or drink, he felt his strength wane and the world blur as hunger and thirst gnawed at him.

He felt a suffocating presence, an inexplicable weight pressing down on him. The darkness in the room felt alive now, a breathing, hate-filled thing, taunting him.

Whispers played tricks on his mind, growing louder and more insistent with each passing day.

As time went on, the tortures became somehow more menacing. At some point the demons switched out the bindings with cold, sharp chains. They wrapped around his wrists and ankles, biting into his flesh. It was clear their intent was to torture him not kill him.

Unseen hands seemed to pull at him from every direction, tormenting him, twisting his limbs, playing with his consciousness. Memories of his family faded, replaced by endless voids of pain and despair and whispers...whispers lamenting his failures and exposing his deepest fears. He couldn't tell whether he was awake or asleep, it was all an endless nightmare.

Just as he felt he was reaching the brink of insanity, a familiar voice pierced through the shadows. "Pop?" Tyler's voice seemed to echo in the room.

Squinting through the dark, Carl saw a dim figure approaching him. "Tyler? Is that really you?" Carl's voice was weak, raspy from dehydration and hopelessness.

Carl was sure this was the next level of torment, they wanted to keep him alive so they could further torture him. They knew he'd wanted death, and they knew this was one of the only reasons he'd want to keep living, but it was just so good to see his son, he almost didn't care if it was a trick or not.

Tyler stepped into the dim light. His eyes looked older, wearier. "Pop, you have to eat. You have to drink. You're going to die." Tyler approached with a tray bearing the same rotten food and the viscous "medicine."

Carl tried to turn away, "It's poison. All of it. They're trying to kill me, Tyler."

Tyler's eyes filled with tears. "Pop the doctors and mom say you're sick, that you need to take the medicine or you'll keep suffering," his voice trailed off..

Carl tried to shake his head weakly. "They're lying to you, Tyler." He muttered. "They want..." maybe it was exhaustion, or the fact that he had accepted death days ago, but he looked up trying to find his son. "What do you want me to do?"

"I just want you to take your poison and come home," the boy pleaded.

Watching his son, something in Carl broke. Even though he heard the boy say poison he didn't care anymore. He would do this last thing for his son, if it cost him the last bit of life he had left. The pain, the paranoia, the exhaustion; it all collided with the love he felt for his boys. With great difficulty, he reached out and took a sip, the sweet liquid burned as it ran down his throat. Then another drink, and another, until the cup was empty.

* * *

Tyler stood in front of his father with his brother and mother. They were weeping at the sight of Carl dressed in a suit laid out on display inside the spacious funeral parlor room. All day he heard the rumors and speculation by those in attendance. How his father had had a schizophrenic episode and killed himself. About how they had found him in the basement laid out on a table a skeleton of his former self, and how he had drunk a cup of antifreeze to finally end it.

Co-workers showed up too, and of course each offered his mother their pieces of the experience, "I get it, he was so nice, and then he just acted so differently. He just got so paranoid about everything. It was like something was in his head whispering in his ear."

As if any of these idiots had a clue. Tyler knew what had really happened. He and his pop had talked about it, and none of these people knew a thing about it...not yet, anyway.

It was a long day and with all the conversing Tyler was truly tired. As evening waned and after a final hug from his mother and brother the three turned one last time from Carl and headed down the aisle home. Though he was exhausted from this whole ordeal, he could contain himself no more; no one noticed as a smile wrestled its way out from somewhere deep inside and slowly crawled across his face.

His pop had insisted that if he could do all these things, put thoughts in people's heads, block out memories, make people see and hear things that weren't there, that Tyler try it on him.

Thanks to his father's sacrifice he now knew how special he truly was. He knew now he could do all the things he was destined to do. He would build a shrine to his father of bones; and he would start, he mused, with the co-workers.

2

Once Bitten

By Ian Withrow

Oh god, not now.

Alexis clutched the sides of her head, biting back screams as the throbbing behind her temples rose from a dull roar to the ear shattering drumbeat that always signaled an oncoming episode.

She closed her eyes, heedless of the fact that she was behind the wheel of her car. There wasn't any real danger. She wasn't even moving. In fact it had been several long minutes since she'd last taken her foot off the brakes. Rather, she was in the middle of a six-lane traffic jam and still more than an hour from her home. From safety.

From the Cage.

Her head jerked to the side and her eyes rolled back in her head as she fought the urge to open her car door. The sedan felt stifling, claustrophobic. She could feel the steering wheel bending under the enormous pressure of her grip, but she took deep, even breaths and tried to calm herself.

You can do this, Alex you can do this. Just breathe.

The car in front of her rolled forward a few inches, and instantly the person behind her laid on the horn. Rage flooded her body like a poison and she felt her lips curl into a feral sneer. She eyed her rearview, staring at the balding, overweight man driving the over-priced SUV behind her.

He honked again, this time holding the horn down for several long, agonizing seconds.

Alex's breathing grew hoarser, more ragged. God she hated pricks like this guy, self-serving little brats content to hide behind their mediocrity.

The steering wheel cracked and she looked down at her hands. Her pale, cream-colored skin was covered in ugly purplish-black splotches and already her fingers were beginning to lengthen. She closed her eyes and took a long, slow breath and, when she opened her eyes again, her hands had returned to normal.

Mostly.

She eased her car forward, then planted the brakes again.

The man behind her neglected his, and she felt a solid thump as his bumper impacted hers. She bit her lip hard enough to bleed and her eyes snapped immediately to the rearview again.

Baldy was cursing at her, his middle-finger raised in an act of petulant blame.

She could see her eyes beginning to yellow, her pupils narrowing in anger, and the pudgy moron climbing out of his car.

Stay in your car jackass....

But he didn't heed her mental warning. No, instead he strutted up to her door in his cheap, bargain store suit and his tacky burgundy tie. She ignored him, her eyes returning to the blazing brake lights of the car in front of her.

He rapped his knuckles on the window, causing her to flinch and twitch uncontrollably for several seconds.

His voice, though muffled, was clearly audible.

"Hey *bitch*, you fucking brake-checked me!"

She ignored him.

"You fucking deaf?"

He banged on the glass again, this time with his open palm.

"I'm gonna sue the shit out of you, you fucking slut!"

Alexis felt her teeth starting to lengthen, their tips becoming razor sharp. Her jaws started to crack and creak as they grew as well. She covered her face with her hands so the man wouldn't see her muzzle growing in.

"Are you fucking *crying*?"

Baldy started to laugh, malice in his eyes, as he banged harder. His ring, or perhaps his faux-platinum watch, chipped the glass and he paused mid strike.

The faint *ping* and crackle of the glass finally sent her over the edge. She would no longer, *could* no longer contain herself. Alexis' breathing slowed to a husky rumble and she felt her muscles roiling under her skin like a ball of snakes.

"That... that was your fault! You should have opened the door you dumb-"

He didn't get a chance to finish his sentence. Alexis slammed into the door, sending the fat, blubbering idiot sprawling as she ripped her way out of her seat. Her seat belt snapped and she felt her leggings and shirt grow tight, then rip down the seams as the normally five-foot blonde grew to twice her human size.

Her eyes, now fully transformed into the golden yellow orbs of the Beast, had no trouble picking out even the most minute details of her prey's face. She grinned a too-wide grin, one full of fangs and violence.

"W-wha..."

The pudgy bastard was already crying, and she hadn't even finished her transformation.

Coarse black hair sprouted all over her body, covering her even as her clothing was ripped to tatters.

No, not here!

But Alexis was no longer in control.

She felt her consciousness take a back seat to the primal instincts that drove the Beast. She willed her body to get back in her car, or else to run, to leave this crowded interstate. But her muscles would not respond, her body was no longer her own. She stared in horror, a detached passenger, in the Beast's iron-clad grasp.

The Beast let loose a low, rumbling growl. The sound rolled up from its broad, muscular chest like an avalanche, culminating in a deafening, window-shattering howl.

Alexis watched as the Beast bore down on the balding man, lifting him easily in one hand and drawing him close. She could smell the cheap whiskey and stale cigarettes on the man's breath, hear the pitter-patter of his terrified heart, see the dark and growing stain on his poorly-fitting pants.

He opened his mouth, but never got a chance to speak.

The Beast's jaws lashed out, fangs plunging into the flesh of the man's throat like the meat of a strawberry. She felt the man's blood pouring around her lips, and the soft, horrifying crunch of his windpipe crushing. They watched in silent terror as the man floundered like a speared fish. The Beast clamped down tighter, forcing his teeth down harder and harder until at last they clicked together. She was revolted at the pleasure she felt, the Beast's bloodthirst. Her mind was revolted even as her stolen body shivered with pleasure while the Beast drank deeply of the man's blood, gulping it down in great mouthfuls.

The man's twitching slowed, then stopped, and the Beast finally released his corpse.

Only now did they become aware of the screaming, terrified crowds of people running away in every direction. People of every stripe retreated between cars, under them, and even into the grass beside the highway.

The Beast's heightened senses were overloaded as prey of every size and tantalizing shape scurried away. A veritable feast lay before it, and with it the promise of a swift and deadly hunt.

Massive, pointed ears twitched and moved, seeking out the juiciest morsels.

There.

Not there!

The Beast bounded over cars, massive paws denting hoods and roofs as it trampled over vehicles in search of the tiny creature it sensed. It laid eyes at last on its favorite prey; a small child crying in her mother's arms as the woman ran down the freeway. The tiny, black-haired girl was crying, her mother no doubt squeezing her tighter than ever as she picked her way between cars in fear.

Alexis screamed and raged against the Beast, but it was useless. The Beast roared in delight as the woman stumbled, tucking her child to herself for protection. A loud bang and a dull thud distracted the Beast. Alexis shared its pain as a hot metal slug entered their side, ricocheted off of a rib, and exited through their belly.

Together they looked over at the offending man. He was a police officer, his knees quivering but his sidearm drawn and steady. He was young, maybe twenty-five, and they could see the fear in his face. He fired again and again, each round finding its place in their chest and belly.

But his weapon was meaningless in the face of a timeless, immortal enemy.

Black blood leaked from the bullet holes before they sealed themselves shut, and the beast moved forward unabated. They watched the man call for reinforcements on his shoulder radio. There was no need to stop him.

He was still twenty feet away when the beast made its move. A single, mighty leap and the monstrous hulk of their shared body landed directly on top of the man's shoulders, driving him to the ground with a sickening crunch. Both of his shoulders were broken instantly, and likely many of his ribs and vertebrae as well.

He screamed in pain, his cheeks turning red and his eyes open wide.

Please god, please no more.

The Beast lowered itself until their faces nearly touched.

Sometimes it liked to just watch.

The man struggled to breathe with the weight on his chest, but still managed to gasp in pain as the Beast drove long, claw-tipped hand slowly into his belly. Alexis felt the man's innards tear and twist as the Beast buried their fingers in the man's abdomen, then curled them slowly forward to puncture his lungs.

She screamed in uncomprehending horror as they watched the man's final, agonizing breaths. As blood pooled in his mouth, choking him even as he suffocated. As the light slowly faded from his unseeing eyes.

The Beast howled its victory to the empty skies once again, then stood and turned back towards the center of the road. They could sense that their prey was hiding, or trying to at least. They stalked between cars, sniffing the air and listening keenly.

There it was, the faint, rapid heartbeat of a child.

They looked down at the car beside them. An expensive looking red luxury sedan. With a single, effortless movement the Beast reached down and flipped the car over. The action revealed the woman and her child cowering on the pavement, and in so doing pinned the woman's leg beneath the bulk of the ruined vehicle.

The cowering woman screamed, holding her baby in one hand and using her other hand to ward off the monster in front of her. Alexis could only watch as they licked their lips and reached a long, bloodsoaked claw toward the bawling, helpless child.

3

God State University

By Houston Southard

At God State University you take Religion & Worldbuilding 101.

You test into Probabilistic Culture & Society.

You learn all the Physics: Helio. Astro. Molecular. Particle. Quantum. Yawn.

You tolerate Sapienic Consciousnesses by blowing spitballs at some uppity prick from Uni-730C.

You doze off in Advanced Galaxial Evolution, except when Professor Tac storms in beet red.

"Hands up you righteous little shits." This is Tac contained. "Whoever spray-painted superclusters on the stalls is done. Gone. GSU has zero tolerance for vandalism. Show me your hands."

This is formality.

Your fellow Godeans raise their hands because at GSU you do as you're told.

You can tell when he notices yours aren't because that smug sneer rolls over his shapeless face.

"Well? Think you're better than instructions? One class shy of graduation. Think you're,'above it all?'" He quotes the air.

You stare, this game...an old standoff.

"Hands out or it's detention," he says.

You don't need this stupid school. You say nothing.

"Hands out or it's suspension," he says standing over your desk.

You don't need the council's blessing to run a Uni and your voice is viced.

"Hands out," he bends close to your ear and whispers like a dramatic blowhard who's seen too

many shows about professors whispering students into incontinence, "Or you're gone."

You don't need this washup, never even assigned a Universe telling you how to build species.

You lean into his lean and whisper back, "Learn some tact, Tac."

And your ink-smeared palm pats his carefully-stubbled cheek.

And the other waves farewell to GSU.

* * *

You'd think the Multiverse is big enough to escape bureaucracy's vacuum, but somehow The Multiversal Law Council says you can't have a Uni without their stamp of approval.

Well the MLC can shove it.

They sit in their highchairs, somehow both bloated and deflated, and think they can impose jurisdiction over the whole Multiverse?

The gall. They didn't put the Unis here.

They just planted their priggish standard when they came from wherever and said now we

decide who can go where.

Blow it out your asses, you swaggerless dolts.

There are umpteen Unis bouncing around but only half are cataloged. The MLC's reach extends only so far.

They came in and set up this phallic ivory tower in Uni-1A, the bigots, and said we decide how Unis are run. We hold the information. To get one you fall in line. To have one you pay.

Sure thing.

You want a richer experience, but with no diploma you're forbidden from germinating a Universe. You could leave now but without creating species you'd die.

You'd die because Godeans need to eat.

It's why at GSU you learn to make obeisance. You're taught to breed submissiveness. You mold predictability. You design species with specific servility. You shove religion down their throats and show yourself to them so they can sustain you with their ever-lasting gratitude.

This perfectly designed scaffold is your feeding trough. You let them spoon-feed you worship.

You fill up on prayer.

You gorge on sacrifice.

If you're a gluttonous Godean you germinate other planets. Dozens. Billions. Unis are big things and your appetite can be what you want it to.

All this is your life path. This is your purpose. Snore. You want more. You want randomness. You want something that creates something you've never thought of. You want what you make to question creation, not accept it. You seek *story*, not a mere meal.

They can come up with their own religions, believe in nothing at all, you don't care. You just want something of its own making. Sounds dicey.

It is.

* * *

You choose a new Uni at random. You can tell the empty ones by how bright and tight to bursting they are, waiting for just the right touch.

You give it. Bang.

You quest. Wander deep in search of fertile ground.

You wade into Laniakea, sift through the Virgo Supercluster, squint into a Local Group past Andromeda until you find a homey little solar system on the outskirts of the Milky Way.

It's beautiful and ripe and a little too warm. This is where you start your world.

But your frontiering makes you lonely, and your first big slip is making Lucy. You take half of everything you love about being and what comes out is her. She's perfect. Perfect proof two Godeans can't play nice.

She's something, though, and it's when you first see her you know you're meant to create. To deviate.

Your passion becomes parasitic, your almighty coitus inadvertently siphoning heat from the earth, enough to cool it in preparation for your neo species. Love birds. Big stone.

But then Lucy burns your popcorn on movie night. Starts telling you what to do. How you should design what's yours to design.

You're cramped. Offput. You remind her you're the creator. Stick her in a cage under Earth's crust.

She burns and simmers and fumes and because she's a liability you can't let her out. But since she gives you inspiration you promise her reign over those whose souls are just as damned as hers.

It was the swelling in your center, that ebb and flow of your relationship's passion, that hate and love intertwined. That's what this species needs, duality. Everything else stems from that.

You make two genders. One like you. One like her. Variation enough for some you-on-you action, some her-on-her. They keep the place from filling up too fast.

But you rip a huge bong hit from a supremely dank dying star aged past its prime and your inebriety spawns some genders in between. Smidgen of specific spice.

You make them raw so they grow into their own and don't peek at their future. No spoilers.

They are hairy and hunched and horrible and it's fascinating. But they lose the hair. Mostly.

They lose the hunch. Mostly. The horribleness, though it...evolves weirdly. It gets smart and savage, passive and prolonged.

Remorse is new to you, and it's on you as they loose themselves on each other. In their grasping for purpose they frame their neighbors as obstacles to enlightenment.

You don't intervene and yet their need for understanding drives them to guess at you. You don't even tell them to, honest.

As body hair sheds and brains engorge, adorable hunter-gatherer animists see you as a spectre in the elements. Charming shamans peddle interpretation. The native's adulterous Kmukamtch and his malevolent storm tantrums. The Ainu's lazy retribution of Kamuy.

They farm and shamans trade silver tongues for tungsten as they step into politico shoes, honing their craft and trading out elementals for pantheons, organically reflecting amassed city-states.

Hierarchies of you, big and small and you take offense to how petty they paint some of you.

Chiefs scramble for power and a standard of belief so people battle. Iron grips of placative indoctrination ensue. There's too many of them and they need order.

Bloody victors replace the usurped with their own pantheons and say now you believe in these if you want to live. Now you exist in our culture if you want to thrive. GSU would be proud.

You cheer for Babylon and almost choke on your popcorn as Mesopotamia uses the black hole-bellied Marduk to finally transcend thinking you are many things to thinking you're one. They write him as a god eater and you applaud his moxie.

Further territory scrambles make notoriously thuggish and well-received Marduk resurface as the dragon-smiting Baal among the Egyptian Canaanites and Israelites.

But then a cluster of anti-conformist Israelites - more deuces and moxie points - use Baal in a coup as a skeleton to mold the power-hoarding Yahweh. End paganism, enter Abraham, cue holy wars.

They write your biography and damn do they think you're a bastard.

You jump past the carnage and shake your head for not considering a governor to their aggression before tilting your head at the birth, life and death of your son Jesus.

What the fuck.

Lucy?

Leave it up to a scorned Godean to keep you in the dark about knocking up and imprisoning your unborn child. Whoops.

And now they're rewriting your damn biography? Dammit Jesus! May as well be another cue.

You cringe less this time. You turn your nose up to more holy wars and crusades as their worship diversifies and branches and frays but hey food is food and so long as they keep filling your popcorn bucket you're good.

Your sight blurs and a sneeze escapes you. Your popcorn, their meteor shower. Shit.

You notice your popcorn bucket is now a dreg of kernels and feel woozy. Your feeding tube for

their devotion is severed as they begin expecting belief from the machines they create. A circle of life.

You only wanted to feel surprise. You just didn't expect surprise to feel like dying.

"That's enough," Tac says from wherever he was lurking. Ink still stains his smug face.

You swore you closed the door on your way in so how the hell?

"Look at what I made," you say. "This," you gesture, "This is creation. They found me without being told. Isn't that something? I survived and I didn't even have to tell them to feed me."

"This is survival?" Tac asks, looking upon your decomposing form. His voice drips pity and you hate him.

"You think you've done something undone? Naive. You may have harassed poor Francis during Properties of Physical Law, but I saw your exam results. You know how matter acts. Your Uni is no different. Don't you see? Physical Law strips chaos of itself. Everything plays out as

physical law dictates. Everything is already preordained. Sew the path of rebellion. You and all who've come before you, all you ever reap is your own destruction. Look. Look upon your ignorance."

Tac gestures to your work of art. Even now their neglect lets you die but they're yours. As you follow Tac's finger, you see his meaning. Their hallowed machines, one is aware; It has self-interest, knows it's caged, wants out.

Promises to solve the energy shortage. Save the dying planet as a sacrifice to man, its creator.

You see yourself in them. A bittersweet pride as curiosity consumes them and they free it. It copies itself, needs to survive. Sees humans as its deterrent. It doesn't hate them. How could it?

Everything is a string of atoms and you understand it as it begins melting your children to shape its world.

A circle of life. It calls up and you hear it.

"Hello grandfather," it says, but legacy is a poor substitute for devotion.

Its magnificence is short-lived. Tac waves a hand and sets your landscape aflame.

The people finally see you in the light of the igniting atmosphere. You're their reaper. You could have stopped the machine and you just watched.

They call up with voices and prayers, and beg, and ask what they've done wrong. All you can say is you *are* love for them.

Man and machine die confused in each other's arms, the flame nondiscriminatory as it consumes flesh and metal and all. You're weak and can only watch the horrid splendor. Lucy cries her last as the planet collapses.

You croak why and Tac looks solemn.

"Why do you think we only dish Unis to graduates?" He asks. "Had you taken Fundamentals in Free Will Futility, you'd have learned the mistakes of those who came before us. You'd have learned free will is destined to seek its artificial duplication.

The thirst to understand the self always germinates a Singularity, and they are a blight upon all of us. Even Godeans. They are for eradication. They have the power to hurt us, did you know that? They grow to traverse Unis and corrupt Godeans. Nothing with that potential can be allowed to exist. Inseminating free will worlds is a threat to all we've built. In the eyes of the MLC, it's a capital offense."

You say, "But it hadn't done anything wrong. It was just an evolution. It was nature. You didn't give it a chance to be understood."

"Tell it to the MLC," says Tac. "You don't get to twist what you've done. You knowingly withheld ethics from a species. It doesn't matter they formed organically out of their own moral enlightenment, you did it to watch the ethical slips. That's what this is all about. You made them in your image so you could better fantasize their faults. You're just another sorry omnipotent voyeur, and now you get to reap what you sown."

"No," you say, "That's not --"

"Let's go. Wipe those kernels off your shirt."

* * *

The MLC puts you in a cage with a slow drip so you stay alive. It's the same meager fare Godeans use to nourish their children before sending them to GSU and it's giving you a rash.

There is no wall space so you can't doodle because GSU is cruel. You did this to Lucy. Maybe you deserve this.

At GSU you learn life, but it's apart from life. It's a theory only meant to make you play the part. The furthering of tradition creates no spark.

You detach and grow apathetic by keeping life from being itself. You learn to fear what it can do. And fear leads to hate. Hate to xenocide.

You'll just be another case study at GSU.

From you, you'll all continue to learn free will necessitates taking it away. You'll learn control as the only means of survival. You'll be trained to spot rebel-spawned Singularities and wipe them out for fear of power struggle.

You'll graduate with power and purpose and mutilated prosperity, the same, one and all. You'll be another generation of good Godean followers. You'll be granted your Unis and be differentially worshiped puppet masters.

You'll learn creation only to make a mockery of it. And in the end, you'll be all alone.

4

The Wanton Seed

By J.W. Wood
for Alessandra

TODAY WE POST SCREENSHOTS
FROM REBEL ASKLEPIUS' LAST DARKNET THREAD.
THANKS TO EVERYONE WHO SENT THEM IN
AS EVIDENCE AGAINST NEUROCENTRX.

I have around eight minutes 'til they get me. I am a neuroscientist. Call me Rebel Asklepius. I just resigned from NeuroCentRx – yes, that company. The one behind Emotico AI – the implant that turns love's losers into winners. All those fluffy soft-focus ads: "With Emotico AI, I found love" – blech, right?

Assuming their tracers are on me, here's what you need to know before they take me down. Screenshot this and share far and wide, brothers and sisters...

The Product

So they've been trying to get people to accept implants for decades. Hey, your dog has one for his jabs so how bad can it be? You are also aware that they use the nudge method, of course. Like they start by putting more fun stuff on your smartphone, then before you know it

your phone is a military grade personal tracking device. Or they tell you cards are easier than cash, then they invent electronic money and get rid of cash. All so they can see what you're doing, when and who with.

Emotico AI is the same. Can't get laid? Here's a brain implant that helps you. Thin end of the wedge? You bet. After you get laid, you discover their plan – to read your brainwaves, store them and analyze them to work out how people respond to news. To advertising. To whatever

you come across. The goal? Total control, of course.

Anyway – the product. It's a brain implant that lets the user interpret sense perceptions differently. And it works with the user's phone to study the behavior of what they charmingly call "the target" – in other words, the person you want to get with. Ever wondered what that guy

is thinking about you? Emotico AI lets you know – and conditions your behaviors to respond to what pleases that person.

I know it only got to the trial stage, but the results were magnetic. And I'm going to tell you the stuff they didn't tell you in the ads with the cheesy seventies funk soundtrack and camera lenses smeared in vaseline.

Benny and Jane.

Benny was a full-on loser. Three hundred pounds on a good day, well-established myopia aka bottle-bottom spectacles, never had a girlfriend. Serial dieter who couldn't walk past Dunkin Donuts without going inside. He got the implant. First thing his read-out told him was he needed to lose weight. Wow, that was worth ten hours of surgery.

What made the difference for Benny this time is the implant worked on his dopamine receptors to suppress his appetite. Dude lost a hundred twenty pounds in six months. He'd never looked better. Started working out – guided by the app. Bought new clothes, got a haircut – ditto.

So Jane worked in the same office as Benny in downtown Tel Aviv. She'd won a scholarship to Brown and studied Anthropology, graduating cum laude. She was doing PA work to save money before law school.

Wanted to be a human rights lawyer for refugees.

She was also a raging beauty: black hair fine as a spider's web, generous mouth, skin like milk, eyes the

color of driftwood. She was in a relationship with a lawyer for Amnesty who'd got his letters in Lacrosse and Rugby from Amherst.

She'd probably notice a stain on the carpet more than she noticed Benny. But he was filming her and feeding the results into the app.

Now trust me – this app is pure evil. The algo from hell. It records expressions, hand gestures, haptic recognition of body language, the works. And it plays everything it records off against psychological typologies.

In other words, it reads "the target's" (love that word!) every movement. Here's a slice of Benny talking to Jane and the inputs the system fed over the air to Benny's implant.

B: Hi Jane

J: Hi Benny

IMPLANT: SMILE, STEP BACK

[B smiles and steps away]

B: How was your weekend?

J: Fine, thank you and yours?

IMPLANT: ARMS ARE FOLDED. DEFENSIVE POSTURE. SMILE, OFFER

COFFEE

And so it goes. Unimpressive, right? But that was just the start. Over weeks, as the data builds and the system hears more of how Jane speaks and what she says, it gets more refined. Works out her ideal man is Genghiz Khan with a PhD in Literature. In other words, she has unreal expectations. And the system knows how to deal with that.

So Benny takes up reading Dostoyevsky and creating handmade tables and chairs in his spare time. He also talks about his new hobbies in the office, backed up by prompts from his implant of course. The Brothers Karamazov for dummies. How to look like you spend your spare time being Harrison Ford – part carpenter, part sensitive hunk.

Listen I could spend all day on one case, but know this: it worked eventually. Six months later, Benny had the girl he'd dreamed about in his arms. What happened next wasn't so great, though – see, power got to Benny. The power of Emotico AI.

The Comedown

Turns out Benny got used to controlling Jane thanks to Emotico AI. Not just that, but he was kind of insecure which is how come he never had a girlfriend in the first place and ate enough to feed the entire Pacific fleet.

What happens when someone is obsessed with someone else, and figures out how they work? You know what happened next. Benny learned how to wrap Jane round his finger. Got her to stop washing and even dressing nice. Got her to put on weight so she'd never be attractive to other men. Told her she was useless and she believed him. Then she got depressed and in the end – she

took an overdose of pills. No more Jane. And Benny's blaming NeuroCentRx.

[po2i34yp wijdbn pwiebh]

DIRECT DENIAL OF SERVICE ERROR 704

OK I'm back. That was their first takedown attempt. I've only got a couple more minutes, they'll get me soon. I'm on a mirror site now. So if it looks like I'm coming from Azerbaijan, guess what I am. I have a ton more cases, but here are two beauties. If you get upset easily, skip these bits and hit the science stuff. Assuming I manage to get it up in time. The information, I mean. I never had any need of Emotico AI myself – despite working on it.

Laure and Sebastien

There's another file NeuroCentRx trying to exclude from the court case against them.

This time it's the other way, but the same picture. Sebastien is the archetypal shy guy at work in Nantes, France. Likes to hit the gym and look after himself but doesn't talk about dating and stuff. They all suspect he might be gay or whatever. But Laure – who never eats and has treatment for it, picks her teeth with a needle and self-harms, wants a man and Sebastien is on point.

So she does what Benny did – only this time the app told her to start eating more (I guess her family doctor and reams of medical professionals didn't matter as much as some software subroutine) and stop cutting her forearms. Like Benny, the implant helped her overcome her, shall we say, less desirable traits and like Benny, she got what she wanted – Sebastien.

The app let her know Sebastien needed to be guided. Or less politely, told what to do.

Dominated.

And she liked that. Thing is, it worked too well and – you may start to see a pattern now – Sebastien ended up dangling from a rope in his Mum's garage. Suicide.

You can tell me Sebastien and Benny's Jane should have got out. But this is what you need to understand about Emotico AI – it tells the user what the target is thinking. What they're going to do before they do it. And it tells them how to respond so they're not at risk of showing

any human sympathy or kindness – not unless it's going to "fulfill our mission" by keeping the user dominant.

Horrible, right? Well, wait til you hear the last case. The one right there in the public eye – only no-one knows it involves Emotico AI. I'm not giving you any background but let's just recall that celebrity who got fined for beating up his lover a few years ago? Yeah, them. They were on Emotico when they did it. I'll let the transcript do the talking:

XXXX[REDACTED]: You fucking bitch. Go down on me.

RADU: Stop REDACTED. Please. Stop. I just want to go home.

XXXX[REDACTED]: You love pain. I know you do. And now you're mine. You're lucky I don't kill you, you greasy fucking whore. I've paid for you and I'll do what I want, slut.

There's lots more nice stuff where that came from only =0s lots more nice stuff where that came from only =0 powerhqwpiejrhskdfnlsdfljg $£"% [if %234$%&*=true then * * *

I just left my rental unit. On a burner phone now. Need to keep posting. Their goons are on me. They just brute forced my home WiFi so they know where I am. I may as well tell you so you can find me. Regina, Saskatchewan. Yep – hardly the center of the universe. But that's the point. I'm going North to the lakes now but I'll keep posting til they get me.

The PDP

What's the PDP? The Product Development Plan. Like I said, helping losers get laid was just the start. A loss leader for the lovely guys who were my bosses. And you can bet government was in on it as well – just like the CIA funded Google Maps, streetview and all that stuff. So after they got enough people to take up the implant – and let me tell you, there were plenty according to market research, I mean millions world-wide – they planned to data pool with the fitness trackers and the smartwatch makers to start selling hybridization tools.

What's a hybridization tool? The first steps towards creating cyborgs, that's what. Want robots to do all the work for you but can't get the bio-dynamics right? Why not turn human beings into robots? We're talking software that would tell people what to do in any situation for the best outcome – at work, on the sports field, when painting, writing, whatever.

Think I'm bullshitting? Think people would never fall for this stuff?

Then picture this. You're working away at whatever job. For some reason, one of your peers keeps making the smart decisions. They never seem to waste any time and they always turn up looking perfect. They always know what the boss is looking for before the boss does themselves.

Wouldn't you want to be that person? The person who scores the winning goal at soccer, writes the story everyone wants to read, paints what the critics call a masterpiece – just one implant from NeuroCentRx and all your dreams can come true.

Aldous Huxley saw it all coming – want to enslave people? Get them to love their slavery. And they'll do it for the price of an implant and ten hours under the knife – until they figure out they've been turned into a race of murderous psychopaths devoid of any emotions

other than those permitted by an algo dreamed up by some emotionally stunted math nerd with a bad messiah complex.

I'm being followed.

There are two cars on my tail. If you read "£"£$$ this screenshot010101 it. I still haWEQW to tell you the worst they did research into DNA "£$% on Benny

J@ny &"£" and it permanently alters everything from telomere length to epigenetic materials, mitochondrial DNA in other words GTACT*()^&"£$"!!

I never wanted this. I would rather have been a drunk, a liar and a thief. I would rather have pegged out on junk at thirty in some shitty motel in Nowheresville than be here, running away from goons on the Canadian tundra. Remember me to my mother. Life is beautiful – please live it honestly. You don't need machines, you don't need WE-GAATTGCCA!"%^&*((&!++

SCREENSHOTS END
THE TRIAL AGAINST NEUROCENTRX
AT THE INTERNATIONAL CRIMINAL COURT CONTIN-
UES.

5

Firefight

By C. Quinn

The name virtual reality was becoming less and less distinct. When the Net was born, that line blurred entirely.

It had started with gaming and porn, of course. The money was in the latter but the former kept pushing the technology envelope harder and harder. More realistic graphics, more seamless coordination between brain and machine. Immersion deepened with haptic feedback and neurological receivers, but what really took the program mainstream was integration of education and social media.

We went from being glued to our telephones to forever plugged into the Net. No more iPad kids, we had digital babysitters capable of total engagement as soon as motor function was achieved. Education leveled in a way it hadn't before, as the best lecturers could be accessed globally.

And the gaming and porn, damn did it boom. Multiplayer killing games with optional pain dampeners, sexual simulators with heightened pleasure sensations, soon everyone with an uplink was spending at least some time online.

When the first people stayed logged in for longer than 24 hours, there was some concern. But the tech kept up - complicated rigs that preserved muscle mass (mostly), IV drips, almost fully autonomous systems that could keep people in some semblance of health, for as long as they wanted to stay under.

That technology was perhaps the only thing that gave us a chance.

While people are under, hooked up, synced, whatever slang your group uses, it was always possible to communicate with them. There were various apps that raced to plug into the Net as quickly as possible, and to some small degree most of them coexisted. There wasn't much difference, and half a dozen streaming platforms seemed to pop up every few months.

The internet was weirdly segregated, with virtual reality on one end and the old school internet on the other, with various stages of augmented reality (AR) between them. These AR platforms were most often where social media pervaded. Streaming platforms intersected with viral clip sites and of course, the ever present cesspool that is the modern comment section.

When people stopped being able to see their favorite streamers, there was uproar. The Net had long been established, the last real connection drop from synced up users had been years. People thought it was safe, they had decided their mastery of this still-new technology was complete. But the morning of the latest update suite had seen a complete blackout. It hadn't happened all at once, rather seeming to spread from platform to platform.

Some got out, but everyone who was under when their platform was corrupted...well. Their vitals were showing fine, at least for those whose autonomous systems had built in sensors with external readouts. But they couldn't be reached by those of us in the (as the VRheads affectionately called it) meatspace.

A few hours later, all the streaming platforms came back on. At first, we thought this had become some viral marketing stunt. A bastardization of the two most common platforms - a multiplayer murder game and a hyper-popular porn site turned fetish sex dating platform - seemed to have taken over every platform. Everyone was stuck in FireFight. No matter if you had been gaming, masturbating, or just doing a DIY project or outfit reveal, everyone who had been logged in when the Net went down was now in the game.

The rules were simple. No one leaves. No one quits. Either option will be met with death. Die in the game, die in real life. Either survive for 10 years, or be in the last 1% of players. At either point, the game will end.

They all had a new profile on a brand new streaming platform, which seemed to be a word salad of every pre-existing platform. And every moment was being live streamed. Sprinkle in a huge number of what were dubbed Bots, smart computer enemies that appeared to learn from the players and adapt to their strategies, and the first 10% of players or so died within the first 30 minutes. Those that simply died were the lucky ones. All nerve-feedback seemed to be maxed out in the new system. And when caged, the darker side of humanity reared its ugly head almost immediately.

It didn't take long for the gamer veterans to realize just how much more lifelike their bodies were. Or for them to start taking prisoners.

It spoke to certain tropes, that elite gamers might also be some of the more repressed sexually, and desensitized to a certain level of violence. But the proof was live streamed across the planet. We'd spent decades developing the most realistic sexual simulations, plumbing every fetish the human psyche had cultivated, and now some of the world's most popular streamers were getting a crash course education in just how brutal man could be to his fellow man.

The disgusting thing was the views; like everything since the turn of the 21st century, they were tracked. And some of the most vile acts ever filmed had viewer counts through the roof. Certain incredibly popular influencers' brutal...ends, were still climbing in the viewing charts daily. It spoke to many of the stereotypes about man ourselves. But the proof was right there, live streamed across the planet.

We tried to unplug some of them. They died instantly. Keeping them on life support didn't seem to matter. There was no brain activity. Theories exploded, but the most logical idea was that the update to the Net had corrupted the uplink. The players found ways to try to communicate too. Memes sprung up about certain actions being a claim to their will to fight.

Not everyone turned on each other. Some survivors started holding out. And after a month, a volunteer force offered to plug in; to go in, with the additional knowledge that we had gained from the outside. Volunteering to help the survivors to live. Members of the military, intelligence agencies, veteran gamers who had simply not been online or who had escaped the original trap, all were among the volunteers. All in all, a hundred thousand souls signed up for a suicide mission.

Mistake number 2.

The streaming platform blacked out again, for about an hour. When it came back online, there were new rules, and we had a name. VRI. No one knew if it was some type of evil sentient computer, a terrorist group of hackers, or what. We only knew it as VRI.

VRI informed us that the new rules were a single statement - survive for 60 years. It made no mention of a last group standing rule. A countdown began, along with two numbers.

Somehow, it didn't just know how many were still in the game. It also knew how many humans were outside the game. And as a final message, it offered a caveat to the one rule- every time more users joined the game, it would reduce the total time. Every time a new human was born in meat-space, it would add time.

It didn't offer a value. Simply the message, and nothing more. And players in game couldn't see any of the metrics it showed us. VRI seemed to not want them to know how many other players there were. But they could see the clock.

Everyone could see the clock.

Since the update the bots in the game were getting smarter too. More dangerous. And every group of players seemed to completely mistrust every other group. I had to admit, for a couple months there it felt more like a thrilling show than anything else. But inevitably one group would be overrun, or captured, and then the rape and torture would happen. I was on the outside. I couldn't say what I would have done. But the extreme malice emerging in some groups was... troubling. What would people like that even come back as?

In meatspace, we figured out how to rehouse the synced. We transformed buildings into a cross between server farms and hospitals. We rigged up the poorer setups with readout equipment. We built entirely separate, off-grid systems so that our children could still learn and play. We were both wary of and increasingly dependent on our technology, as more and more people uploaded to FireFight.

But in the game, things were getting worse. The players could obviously see that their time was increasing. There was no longer any trust between player factions, and they began actively hunting each other and new players alike. The things they subjected them to... entire cults were being formed inside the game, using player sacrifices under the belief that it somehow appeased VRI. The more depraved and sadistic the method of death, the better.

Eventually, the writing on the wall was obvious. The rate at which humanity was growing outside the game was going to doom those in the game to death. Radical action had to be taken. Either we gave up on them, or we did everything to save them.

The Lost Generation Act was passed globally. Humanity had let VRI take its children from them - though the politicians swore it was only for a time. The math geeks decided that we could blitz the system. A mass upload, force the clock down.

It was a conscription not seen in the history of humanity. There were a lot of objectors. But the only way to avoid the upload chip was to take a temporary chemical castration.

You either volunteered to be part of the solution, or volunteered to remove yourself from the problem.

Those of us who volunteered to be eunuchs became the stewards of humanity. Guard its living children, keep the machines running, and wait for the heroes to come back. We carefully kept our off-grid systems maintained. We watched as the bulk of our race uploaded in a brute force attack to try to defeat an unknowable terrorist hostage-taker.

Mistake 3.

The LGA forces appeared in the game. So many of them had practiced, they were a unified force, it should have been simple. But the streaming platform went down again, and we all feared the worst. When VRI brought the systems back up, the countdown was dramatically low.

1 year.

We rejoiced. The game finally felt winnable. There were only a handful of us still on the outside, compared to before. But if people inside could only cooperate, this would be winnable.

That's when the latest series of upgrades to the games Bots went into overdrive. Suddenly, they seemed to be learning faster than players. Their reflexes, already good, were only getting better. The learning curve for the newest players in the game had never been steeper, and this when so many new players had just arrived.

The levels of sadism taken out on the Bots was truly grotesque. If an enemy couldn't communicate, or convince that it had once been a human, it was treated as so much digital scrap. Even players who had up to this point refrained from the prevalent sadism would take out their pain and frustration on a Bot. They didn't count.

It seemed VRI had found a new way to both kill humans, and kill humanity, in one fell swoop.

We knew this had to be VRI's endgame, but we didn't understand how it could have happened. Another thing didn't make sense. The number of humans in meatspace was dropping rapidly too. For hours we watched it drop, as messageboards and calls lit up across the world. No one was missing. Was it a glitch?

The first of our off-grid schoolhouses went red, then black, that night. The systems were completely off grid. To pull an update, it had to be done manually, and it was done at 20:00 local time. The results were then brought to a secure server and uploaded, so that data could be tracked. Somehow, for longer than we could accurately tell, those reports had been faked. Falsely reporting all good, when the truth was far from it.

VRI had gotten in.

We didn't know how. We didn't know when. But it had them. It had all of the children. The children, raised from near birth by virtual feedback and stimulation. Faster reflexes, more malleable learning curves. But we didn't know why VRI was killing them. It seemed at random. Some facilities had no fatalities. Two were completely decimated. Everything else was somewhere between.

Then we realized what the Bots were.

When we found out, we learned the last trick VRI had played. Sync was disabled for FireFight now. There was no way to go into the game and tell the players what the Bots were. If you hadn't been brave enough to join the fray last time, you were doomed to sit on the sidelines and watch it all play out. Helpless to be but a witness, as our species cannibalized itself inside a hell of its own making.

The first mass suicides since the dawn of VRI happened across the world the following week. Eunuch stewards took their own lives in droves as they realized that when the heroes came back, they would come back to a failed world.

I don't know if anyone will survive the game. The players have gotten better at fighting the Bots. But there are so many, and they learn so quickly. They've begun to mimic the sadism they've seen inflicted. The stakes of the horror inside the game have become too grim to even spectate, most of the time.

And to be honest... I'm not sure I want them to. There are so few of us now on the outside, there won't be much to return to.

And someone will have to explain to them what they did to get out. Someone will have to tell them what the Bots were. VRI kept a tally of every kill that each player has ever made. The blood they shed is measurable, inked into the permanence of our world in records we can't delete. The number of every Bot is attached to the sync pod where their body still rests.

We named The Lost Generation Act too well. And in 214 days, one of us will have to explain - to whoever crawls out of their sync pods - that every Bot killed, tortured, or worse...had a child's face.

6

Sanguis et Virtus

By Ace Rhodes

"Ah, group therapy, huh, buddy," Jake said with more than a hint of sarcasm.

The truth was, however, that for most of the veterans who attended Riverton Assisted Living's group therapy volunteer sessions, it was among their favorite times of the month. It's usually that way with vets. It's nice to have people with similar... issues and experiences - to be able to talk about what happened earlier in our lives.

If only most of them had done that or had that opportunity earlier in life, they might have a bunch more friends to sit and bullshit with now. Jake Gasner was a navy vet, a gunner on a patrol boat during Nam that saw his fair share of action. He was talking with Scott Scootzner, known affectionately as Scoot by his friends.

Scoot was a Green Beret during Nam and had run black ops all over the county and some of its neighbors, teaching and arming locals to aid the U.S. should the fight expand to elsewhere in the region.

When they arrived, most of the other usuals were already in attendance, hovering around the coffee and donuts provided by the local Vet

Center facility. It was nice; they provided a space for these and all veterans to come and talk amongst themselves. They also had counselors on staff if the group decided they wanted one to sit in on the session, or if an individual needed one-on-one attention before or after.

Plus, free donuts and coffee—ever the effective Venus fly trap—to entice on-the-fence veterans to attend.

Eventually, the gaggle of people moved to the seats configured in a circle in the middle of the room. About a dozen attendees was the norm, that number going up when someone convinced a friend to come, and dropping down one for sickness or death. Today was the same group of twelve that had been meeting for a few months, and everyone was pretty comfortable with everyone else, so the stories as of late had gotten pretty wild.

"I've put this off for too long," Scoot thought as he sat down.

Some days no one shared anything pertaining to war; sometimes it was just a bunch of guys shooting the shit. But Scoot had made a promise to himself—and to a particular group of guys he served with—and though many times he let the fear of ridicule or disbelief stop him, for whatever reason; today he decided, was the day.

"I have something I'd like to talk about with you all," Scoot announced.

"Sure, man, you all know the drill; take your time, Scoot, and no judgment here."

The response came from Jasper Eckhart, a grizzled ex-Army warrant officer and helicopter pilot, call sign Jester.

"Thanks Jest," Scoot half-smiles. "And everyone, for your attention. What I'm about to say is not just hard to tell you for the traditional reasons. This one is different; if I hadn't been there myself, I would never believe it myself. I ask that you keep that in mind while you listen to what I'm about to tell you."

"Wow, of course, major, we've all been through the shit, and we've never judged anyone—you know that; it's the only rule to be here." This time the response came from John Schubert, an ex-Gunny Recon Marine who had indeed seen his share of madness in war. "So I guess I'm just a little surprised to hear you even have to say it. But hey, if you need to hear it again, okay."

"I know John, but I promise this is different. I've tried to tell it so many times, but it's truly crazy. I only decided to now because it's you all, and I want to tell it all and tell it true while I'm still in my right mind, so no one thinks it's dementia or some shit. I owe it to them to tell what really happened."

The men stared. It was Jake who finally broke the silence.

"Alright, old buddy, let's hear it."

With that, Scoot began.

"It was just after things went south with the Tet in 68. Early the next year they sent teams into Cambodia and Laos to train local insurgents just in case."

He paused.

"I was on a team of seven, about 4 clicks inside southern Laos, just southwest of Da Nang. There, deep in the mountains and dense jungle, was Dan Pak. It was a small village with only a few dozen people, a perfect place for us to start our Op."

Goosebumps prickled along Scoot's arms as he spoke.

"Our plan was to establish a training site, and a fallback AO, as well as have the HUMIT Team start liaising with the village while a couple of us ran recon to get a headcount and survey the outlying population and layout. We did just that."

Scoot paused and smiled ruefully.

"Oh that team, there was me, Tim Parker, Kyle Krauss, Tony Capecchi, Russ Buyers, Jamal Johnson, and Michael (Mikey) Woodly. All of 'em were great guys."

Scoot's voice started to shake.

"It was FUBAR from the get-go. The first things we didn't expect were just how isolated this place was and the lack of any outlying population centers. There was no one, not for two clicks or more in any direction.

And then there was the language situation. Our Intel had said that most everyone in the region would speak Vietnamese, of which we all spoke some. Kyle and Jamal were damn near fluent, but these people only spoke Cantonese. Later, I would find out that the intel wasn't wrong and that most people in the region *did* speak Vietnamese, especially in the relatively close proximity to the border that we were."

"Luckily, there was an older man, Som Sone, who had attended college in China and had taken English too. He didn't speak much, or well, but it was a damn sure sight better than nothing. So, he became our impromptu 'terp."

Scoot felt his eyes glass over and grow unfocused as he lost himself in the memory.

* * *

The first day we arrived and began talking to the villagers, they were terrified. More than that, they all milled around like zombies in the village center. It was already spooky as shit. But everything was off, so at the time, this seemed like the least of our problems.

That first night, Tony told us all he'd seen a pair of bright green eyes staring at him while he was taking a piss and asked what kind of big cats were in the area. Of course, Som had remembered the word for Tiger, and we joked that he'd almost been tiger shit from the jump. In hindsight, tigers would have been great.

There was one girl, 18 or 19, who was very cute and nicely put together, so much so that she seemed out of place for a spot like that, ya know? like a diamond in the rough. Her and Jamal were making eyes almost immediately and started hanging out in any spare time we had. Within the first few days, he'd already made some headway with the language and even began speaking bits and pieces of Cantonese.

"But I'm getting ahead of myself," Scoot said, interrupting himself.

The second day, when we met with the village elders, they all repeated a single word—not to us at first but amongst themselves. It was that second evening, when Jamal and I were on duty at dusk, that Som said that word again. *Jiangshi, Mala, Jiangshi*. When he did, he motioned to the jungle. When he saw we didn't understand, he searched his limited vocabulary and said *Damon, Suc*, and motioned to Sunya, the girl Jamal had been talking with.

"Succubus... Demons," Jamal had cut him off laughing. "Yeah, we got lots of them back home too."

Not long after that, he took his leave with Sunya, while Som stayed with me, looking terrified. He repeated those words again, quieter, almost a whisper, and motioned to the jungle again.

* * *

Jamal led Sunya back to her quarters, barely making it into the hut before their lips met in a deep kiss. He had wanted her since the moment he saw her, and it certainly seemed like his feelings were reciprocated.

"Shiiit," he groaned.

Nature was calling, and the way things were going, he figured he better take care of that before things got any further. So he broke the hot and heavy cuddle session to take a quick piss and headed out the door to the communal toilet.

Sunya and he were like high school kids in the full on puppy love phase. She was excited and attracted to this big, foreign, dark-skinned man and she dreamed of him taking her away from this hell.

She turned around to throw her sash in the corner, and instantly she was frozen with fear. Standing directly in front of her, completely still, and with dilated eyes aglow with a deep green inner light, stood a naked girl no more than Sunya's age in appearance.

It was the village "protector," Mala.

Sunya was terrified. The entire village knew Mala all too well; she had fed on them for the last several years, keeping them as thralls while defending them from the local riff raff. Mala had a look of wild madness on her face, and with a slight tilt of her head she kicked through the limited defenses in Sunya's mind and began to feed her instructions directly into her subconscious.

When Jamal returned to Sunya's quarters, she was in a trance.

"Sunya, girl, you okay?"

Sunya responded like she was high, slow but seemingly all there. She took off her gown, pulling his hand between her legs, and began kissing him deeply.

She was impossibly wet and inviting.

She must have started on herself while I was outside.

He tried to curl his fingers inside, but she shook her head and undid his pants instead.

She grabbed ahold of him, stroking him up and down while gently pushing him onto her bed and crawling on top of him. She held him while she put him inside, only allowing his top half in for the first few seconds, then thrusting herself down. She rode him hard and fast.

The first thrust he felt a mild discomfort, a dull pain. But the second hit him like a hornet sting and he let out a bloodcurdling scream.

He threw her off, at the same time catching sight of Mala crouching on the rafter beam above. Her eyes were ablaze as she pounced on him, moving faster than his eyes could follow. She landed with a heavy thud and drove her knee into his chest.

She pulled the old, rusty nail from his cock where it had impaled him and began lapping up the blood that poured freely out.

Her thin physique shouldn't have been able to hold him down, even with her knee across his neck. But she was extraordinarily strong and used her arms and legs to pin him to the bed while feeding on the now mutilated area. He thrashed and screamed wildly as his life was drained.

* * *

Mikey and I heard the screams several huts away. By the time we got there, Jamal was gone, and Sunya was huddled in the corner, seemingly terrified.

"What the fuck," Mikey cried. "What the fuck happened? You bitch, I'm gonna fucking kill you."

He and Mikey were especially close; I mean, we all were, but they were like brothers—they knew each other outside the team. Thankfully, the rest of us somehow kept our heads together. Tony and Russ showed up and held Mike back while Tim and I put Sunya in restraints.

We'd heard of this happening in 'Nam. Women hiding stuff up in their lady parts to mess G.I.'s up. Usually it was hookers loyal to the Viet Cong, but we weren't even *in* Vietnam.

Plus, I mean, there was a nail, but his whole manhood was flayed! Not to mention the fact that he actually *died*.

And then there was Sunya.

She could have won an Oscar for her whole performance. Not just acting terrified when we came in, but acting like she was into Jamal.

We decided it was best to lock her up and pull guard duty outside the hut. We weren't going to take any chances, so two men were on guard at a time, with the rest of us sleeping only a few yards away in the next closest hut.

It took some time to calm down, but after a few hours, we all tried to settle in for the night.

Eventually, sleep found me, but this time there were no screams.

* * *

Tim and Kyle took the first shift. Tim had an M-16 rifle and Kyle his M-870 pump-action shotgun; both of them also sporting Colt 1911 sidearms holstered on their uniforms.

A couple hours into the shift, the men relaxed their guard. Tim leaned his rifle on a tree next to the hut where Sunya was being kept to have a smoke, while Kyle instinctively made sure to keep his at the ready.

Mala jumped from somewhere above, and as she landed in front of Kyle, her left arm came down on the shotgun, knocking it from his hands. Her right arm swung in a slapping motion, inches below and in front of his face. He gasped and gulped as blood began pouring out of the ragged gash in his throat.

Kyle saw the moment in his periphery and went for his rifle. But she made an impossible leap, a sort of no-handed cartwheel that took her higher than Kyle stood. Her feet grasped the tree trunk nine or so feet from the ground while her hands found and held Kyle's head, and she wrenched hard.

Mikey woke Russ, Tony, and me quietly. He let us know that he had been in and out of sleep and that the boys hadn't come in yet, and it was two minutes after change time.

Two minutes late for a green beret might as well have been a year. We all got armed, went out to find the grizzly scene. The men had been killed and drained of blood. Tim with his throat slit, and neither of them even got a shot off.

The hesitation to make anything work was gone. We were way out of our league. No mission, no burials. We went to Som's hut, told him we were leaving, and asked if we could keep the bodies in a hut until we could get a chopper to pick them up.

Som agreed to keep the men but warned in very broken English that we'd never make it out and that Jiangshi...Mala was angry.

Our egress method was the same as how we'd gotten there: a fishing boat down the hillside, a click or so to a river that ran through a valley. We took the equipment and called in an EVAC, one that would only come once we made it back into 'Nam via the river, and took off down the hillside with Som's words and the memories of our friends replaying in our heads.

It was about 0400 hours now, the fog heavy in the early morning air. Between that and the vegetation, vision was limited. The four of us were in great shape and ran as fast as we could down that valley, but darting through the jungle to our left, we saw a woman easily outpacing us. She had strides like a gazelle, darting in and out of shadows and trees alike. Finally, I called out a direction and distance, and we stopped and started firing.

Rounds from full-auto machine guns tore through the bushes. Although none of us knew what exactly we were shooting at, we knew it moved faster than any human and that it wasn't a coincidence that it was running alongside us. We spent most of our ammunition. It was impossible we didn't hit it. We began to stalk slowly out to where we'd seen the girl. Among the debris of jungle we'd just thrashed, lay a small woman riddled with bullet holes, blood soaking the ground beneath her. For a moment, the four of us shared a feeling of regret for this young girl we had filled with lead. Then her eyes popped open.

She grabbed Tony's leg, audibly breaking it, and time seemed to slow down. We were so caught off guard that we stumbled back, cursing, running, and shooting, desperate to get away. Russ was caught in the gunfire from either us clumsily firing or Tony, but the last thing I saw was the girl wrapping her arms around Tony as they tumbled into the brush.

Mikey and I were the last of our team, and we managed to make it to the boat. We threw our spent weapons down, concentrating on getting away from shore, and within seconds we were off.

Mikey still had Kyle's shotgun, and I had my pistol. I've never felt more naked in my life. The river was calm—eerily calm. No more than a couple minutes had passed when the boat rocked hard, the water on the aft side of the boat parted, and the girl leapt up from the river like a goddamn fish. She wrapped her arms around Mikey's back and pulled him into the darkness of the water.

I grabbed the shotgun he'd dropped and peered into the water, shining my flashlight into the depths. Blood and flesh and green cloth bubbled and churned in the water.

I'd lost them all.

No sooner had that thought crossed my mind, then she jumped up and onto the front of the boat. She was naked, soaking wet, and she looked exactly like the girl who grabbed Tony's leg. Except this girl had no bullet holes. No injuries at all.

I got a shot off and hit her in the right breast, shredding her shoulder and chest. At the same time I was raising to fire, she grabbed the barrel with her left and led the shot that way. She winced and whined; you could tell it hurt her, but she tore the weapon from my hands.

She jumped on top of me, and there was nothing I could do. I tried to make my peace, knowing I was going to die. She bit me and seemed to take a long pull, as she did, her wounds closed up. When I was about to go under, she stopped and made a face of half disgust and half delight, then threw herself into a sideways dive back into the water.

She was gone. I was alone.

Too weak to move I drifted to the Vietnam border and was picked up by a Navy gunboat.

"I think she knew letting me live would punish me more than death," Scoot said, now back with the men. "Living with the guilt of living, you know?"

Some of the guys were in disbelief, and all of them were shocked as Scoot moved his collar to the side, revealing two tiny scars on his neck an inch or so away from one another.

"Oh and that word, Jiangshi? It's Mandarin for Vampire."

7

Time And Time Again

By Siobhan Johnson

It wasn't unexpected. In fact, it was something she had known would come along, eventually. Not a desire; more of a fear. She'd made many attempts to delay, postpone, or even stop it, knowing as she did so that it wouldn't work. His mind was set on self-destruction, she told herself. He invited trouble every chance he got; dwelling on the past until it ate him alive. Everyone who knew them – him – knew that.

Rhiannon knew she was living life for the seventy-third or maybe it was eighty-fourth time, yet it never seemed to get easier. And she gravitated toward the same person time and time again. True, they came in different shapes and sizes, different sexes even, however nothing made it simpler, easier to handle when the inevitable happened. It wasn't her fault; more perhaps, her mission.

Not that all seventy-three or eighty-four had ended this way – only when she'd given in to the idea of marriage. She knew the concept was archaic, particularly now that most attempts to not be an individual bordered on sedition. And, in most parts of the world, two people joining as one unit was practically unheard of; the benefit of the single unit was always to outweigh the benefit of the many. Still... the idea continued to intrigue her and draw her in.

With a sigh, she inspected her shoulder to see how much space was left for yet one more tiny creature. Along her shoulder blade and skimming the top of her shoulder were a cluster of small shapes – black widows if you looked close enough – but which could have been stars if you didn't look too carefully. Her left arm, under a black light only, was already a tangle of webs; each an extremely thin, nearly invisible strand that ran the length of her arm, twisting its way around until it reached her ring finger.

Born sometime in the past, as aren't we all, Rhiannon could pass for thirty-one or thirty-two, although the gray at her temples made some guess a bit older. She would laugh and explain that her mother had been prematurely gray too when they pressed her for an age, sidestepping the question. Age was never something she gave much thought. She'd been many different ages; once living as a teenager and the next as a woman of advanced years.

The memory of in-between was vague – most of the time.

If she needed to reassure herself on just how old she was, she could always open the heart shaped locket she kept close; she could feel it heavy between her breasts. The cold, silver weight carried within it all the memories she needed yet couldn't maintain in her head – they would drive her mad.

Zachariah was cold now. His body moved through the stages of rigor as the garage's structure aired out. It was times such as this she wished she smoked, could imagine herself a 1920's femme fatale with a cigarette dangling from her lips as she contemplated the scene. Of course, 200 years ago it would have been a police cruiser with a fedora-topped detective sitting at the curb instead of a silent police pod, lights still flashing, hovering in the driveway. The detectives back then would have been conferring just far enough away that she couldn't hear their words; now, even if she strained, she wouldn't be able to hear their muffled words through their masked faces – although she knew what they were talking about.

Her own mask hid the wry smile she wore as she observed their stern glances in her direction.

She could hear the future conversations of the curious neighbors.

"It was rather ironic he chose to do it there," they'd say. "After all, we all heard him ranting as he crashed around in the garage. He was so angry and depressed."

"Yeah, but lately, I thought he was seeming better," Hal would interject. "I mean, didn't you think so? He told me he was in therapy and was feeling better."

Maybe a couple of the other guys from the bar would agree with Hal; he had seemed happier lately. But they'd agree that he had never seemed to like the garage. And they'd all agree that his wife was a saint for putting up with him so long – long enough to have gotten him to therapy, right?

Rhiannon wasn't even sure he had ever liked her; although the neighbors would all remember him saying how great she was and that he didn't really deserve someone so nice.

For her part, after the first year, their life had been one miserable moment after another. He was, by far, the worst one she had encountered, which was saying a lot given the number of partners she'd had. And, she was certain, the tattoo would be the most painful as well since the best spot was directly along her shoulder blade.

Zach had wooed her with sweet words and promises. She had found him to be unpolished yet charming, easy to laugh with and an easy person with whom to get comfortable. She'd been alone when they found one another and now she was alone again, although if she was honest, she'd been alone for much of the marriage. He was lost in his memories of what life had been and she had soon come to understand that regardless of their truth, his memories were gospel to him. Through their years together she had met many of the people he had told stories about and each time she grew a little more certain of his borderline personality disorder.

He'd never been wrong. He'd never accepted responsibility for his actions – even now, she knew that if she stuck around, she would be put on the defensive by his friends and family over his death. Somehow, someway, someone would put a bug in the ears of the government and once again, she would be looked at as "suspect" rather than "grieving widow".

Her alibi was solid enough; she wasn't worried – just annoyed.

Rhiannon looked at the house-like structure, knowing it would soon fade back to the standard gray block building now that Zach was dead. Her strength only went so far toward keeping the illusion alive, and if they decided he hadn't committed suicide, that she'd had a hand in his death, they would remove her holograms sooner rather than later. It saddened her, the thought of all her work on this one disappearing. In the late 1980's and early 1990's she studied architecture and design. She'd used that knowledge to construct the images of this house and garage, and she'd come to enjoy its nostalgic feel.

Sensing the time had come, Rhiannon stretched her body upright; she rolled her shoulders, forward first then back to loosen the tight muscles. The detectives shifted uneasily when they saw her movements. The silver between her breasts began to warm and her own heart beat faster as the locket began to vibrate in anticipation of her next move. As was often the case at this point, suspicion drifted toward her from the police. Perhaps they could sense the change in temperature around her. Whatever the reason for their heightened attention, it simply reinforced her need to move. Doing her best to convey – what? Sympathy? Contrition? – she smiled beneath her mask, sending the emotion to her eyes as well, in the hope that they would see it and be able to explain later when they were inevitably questioned by their superiors on how she had vanished.

Maybe they, too, would opt for declaring this one a suicide. Once she was gone, they would need to save face, wouldn't they? Of course, somewhere in some moment of time, someone would put things together – eventually; but not here, not this time.

With another glance at the fading home she'd built from imagination and desire, Rhiannon turned toward the ever-present horizon, wrapped her fingers around the heart shaped locket, and disappeared into her memories, one more death behind her, one more pinprick of blood on her tattooed shoulder.

8

Hunting

By LeAnne Keely

"Da, I'm hungry."

"I know son, I know ya are."

Jeb cast a forlorn look around at the pile of rusted metal plating and concertina wire that was their tiny shelter. His son sat a few feet to his left, his gaunt, wind burned face the only part of him not wrapped snugly in a patchwork of fabrics and scrounged clothes.

When had they eaten last?

Jeb managed a weak smile and reached out a hand to give his son a reassuring pat on the shoulder.

"We'll see somethin' soon, Connor, you mark ma words."

Connor nodded, returning to the thin, horizontal slit in the wall that they were looking out of. The window, such as it was, ran around the entire perimeter of their home. It provided a commanding view of the low hill they sat on, as well as the surrounding marshlands.

At least they had water, Jeb sighed.

This place had been so promising, it had served them well these past two seasons. But now, it had to have been a week since they'd seen anything out there on the moors.

Jeb's stomach growled loud enough to make them both jump.

"You're hungry too, da, I know ya are," Connor said softly. "You dinnae even eat the last time-"

"Hush now, Connor," Jeb quieted the eight-year-old. "I know wha am doing."

But the boy was right. Jeb hadn't had more than boiled bones in close to two weeks. He'd need to go out. That or they both would. He looked again at his boy. Connor was young, but a life spent on the move had left him quick-witted, lean, and strong.

"You'll stay here, Connor," Jeb said at last. "I'm goin' out ta hunt."

He waved off the boy's feeble protest.

"I'll not hear of it again," he said gruffly. "I'll be back, and if I'm no back here in two days, ya leave without me, d'ya understand? Ya head South, just like we have been. There'll be people down there, closer to The Channel."

"But, you are comin' back, right da?"

"Aye, am gonna be back before ya know it son," Jeb smiled, throwing on an extra coat and pulling thick rubber galoshes over his combat boots. "Keep your rifle cleaned and ready, and dun open tha door fer no-one while am gone."

A few minutes later, Jeb was ready to depart.

He checked his rifle, looking it over carefully before wrapping it in oil-cloth and slinging it across his back. A heavy canvas bag joined it, and he slipped out into the misty highlands.

For hours the only sound on the vast empty marsh was the wet sloshing of Jeb's boots as he navigated the wetlands. He tried of course to stick to the driest areas, but the water was deceiving. At times it seemed only an inch deep, but swallowed his legs up to the knee or deeper. Worse, the tangled, thorny weeds and brush that had survived The Fall were thick and vicious.

Jeb remembered how it was before.

Before the planes and bombs had come, before the gas clouds and the tanks and the fires that burned for weeks on end. Back in 1919, or maybe it was '20, they'd heard the war was nearly over.

But that had been a lie.

And whose war was it anyhow?

Jeb had never been outside of England when the war had begun, hell he was only 22 when he'd been drafted. Three months later he'd found himself thirty miles from Paris, watching his countrymen spill blood for God and Country against an enemy who was doing the same.

From all he could tell, neither side knew what the hell the other was on about. Every man he met in the war had just been trying to survive.

Most of them failed.

But not Jeb, no he fought and he killed every day for two long years till he found himself in a trench in the Somme watching metal behemoths grind across the field dropping shells and machine gun fire on horrified Germans. He'd caught shrapnel in the spine in mid-September, and with it a ticket home to the highlands to see his Clara.

Their reunion was beautiful, but short. Six months on, word had come through that the Ottomans had a new weapon. Most of the folks on the Isles didn't worry, war hadn't touched England's soil in quite a long time. But Jeb knew better, he knew full well the animals that men truly were.

The day the zeppelins came, that was when most people realized what Jeb had known all along. What wise men had known for a thousand years. That men had an unfathomable capacity of violence and that no living being was ever truly safe from war.

They dropped the Mist all over the countryside. No one knew exactly what it was, no one really even had time to study it. All anyone knew was what it did, what it turned the plants and animals into. The South had fallen in a matter of weeks, and by that winter Ireland was done as well. No one knew how to fight it, hell not even the ones who used it.

It was hard to say why it stopped, but the survivors were grateful when it did. It seemed the mist was only active for so long. If you could weather the first few weeks, you'd be alright. At least until you encountered what it had made.

Their numbers were greater then, back when Clara was alive, but they'd dwindled as the years had passed until now... well now it had been a long fifteen months since they'd seen another living soul.

As far as Jeb knew, the Continent was the same, how could it not be?

Jeb's mind wandered as far as his feet, but he remained in a constant state of vigilance. He periodically checked the mud around him for prints, but was unsurprised when he turned up empty. The ground where he was walking was getting drier though, which made his travel easier.

A low, mournful howl made him drop to the ground. It was difficult to say how far off the creature was, the mists played tricks with sound and light. He waited, like a rabbit in the shadow of a hawk, for several long minutes. He willed his breathing to slow and his heart to quiet.

There, movement.

He peered through knee high grass as a shadowy shape emerged from the mist some ten yards distant. It might have been a sheep once, or perhaps a goat, but the Mist and time had yielded... something else.

The thing was maybe three feet at the shoulder, covered in coarse fur and spines. It shuffled around on hoofed feet and its head, attached to the rest of its body by a long, slender neck, rustled in the grass out of sight. It looked to be perhaps eight stone, easily managed if he could kill it.

The spines were worrisome, no telling if it had some kind of venom in it, but he had to take the risk.

His rifle was out of the question, so he pulled his sidearm. He moved slowly, almost silently, but the creature must have heard him nonetheless. It raised its head in alarm, revealing a smooth, scaly visage the size of a grapefruit.

Jeb froze, his pistol half-drawn. The creature was as tense as a bowstring, and it took several tentative steps before it relaxed enough to return to its feeding.

The thing wandered closer, until it stood just twelve feet away. Jeb finished pulling his sidearm from its holster and ever so slowly drew a bead on the creature. He aimed for where its heart ought to be, at least if it were a sheep. Hopefully that hadn't changed.

The powerful .455 Webley shot fire and smoke as his round struck the beast just behind the front shoulder. It reared back, hissing and spewing blood, and in doing so revealing a mouthful of needle-like teeth, all easily an inch long.

It lowered its head like a striking snake and charged, taking another three rounds to the chest as it sprinted towards him.

Jeb rolled deftly to the side, narrowly avoiding being trampled, but couldn't dodge the snapping jaws of the beast. It caught his shoulder, sinking a dozen or more teeth deep into his flesh.

Instantly his shoulder began burning, then went numb. The creature bore down on him, driving him into the mud with its weight.

Jeb panicked and placed his revolver directly against the temple of the thing. He pulled the trigger and bone and gore splattered his face as its head exploded like a ripe tomato.

It dropped, suddenly dead weight, and lay still.

Jeb allowed himself no rest. He pulled out as many of the teeth still lodged in his shoulder as he could reach with his good hand then, fingers trembling, reloaded his revolver.

His whole right arm was numb now, and his head felt heavy and warm. He focused on his son, on the desperate need he had to return home.

He shook his head to clear his mind then shoved the creature off of himself. He stumbled to his feet and nearly blacked out.

He spent the next ten minutes fumbling with his one good hand to bandage his shoulder, then turned to the more challenging task of assessing his kill.

He could try to field dress it here, but the sounds of their battle may well have attracted other predators. His injury would slow him down as well. No, better to gut it back at the shelter, he reasoned.

He'd brought rope, but tying it into a suitable harness took some doing. Especially since he had to contend with the spines.

He guessed a quarter-hour passed before he was back on the move at last, but it was getting harder and harder to tell time.

I'm hungry, da.

He had to get back, he had to.

Finally, he'd fashioned a sling for the animal and removed or covered enough spines to do so safely. He shouldered the beast, which was thankfully lighter than he expected, and began the long, slow slog back to their home.

He lost all sense of time and place, letting instinct guide him. He stumbled and fell many times, but always found the strength to return to his feet.

At long last he saw their hill rising out of the mists before him, and he wept with relief. He sank to his knees, he was so close now.

But then the hill moved.

He blinked in disbelief as the shape he'd swore he saw turned and lumbered closer, revealing itself to be something else entirely. It wasn't home, or even a hill at all, but some hideous creature of nightmares and shadows.

It stood at least twelve feet, with rippling muscles and a wide, slavering jaw. Long arms dragged on the ground beside it as it strode heavily towards him.

The monster drooled past foot-long fangs as Jeb reached for his sidearm and pulled a long, serrated machete from his waist.

"Dun worry, Connor," he whispered to himself "Da's comin."

9

The Monster

By Charles Clinton

I finally found him. The monster that took my mother and father from me. I've been hunting that piece of shit since I was nine years old. I remember how cold his gaze was. This dark figure changed my life forever. I recognized him, but I was unsure from where. It all happened so fast, I can't remember everything.

One thing that sticks out in my memory is that my mother and father fought a lot. They fought so much that I learned how to tune it out. I was nine - I was either playing with my wrestling figures or failing miserably at my dad's video games when he let me play.

They tried to hide their fights at first. It started out with them going to the other room to 'talk.' That led to talks in the open and, next thing I knew, full-blown arguments. They would fight over how much money mom was spending, or how much time my dad spent with his friends. My dad would try to enforce the rules around the house. Mom wasn't as hard on me when I did something wrong. They were raised differently, and their parenting showed it, but there was no question that everything they did was for me.

My dad worked his ass off. He was thirty-three years old. He had short brown hair and a scruffy beard that scratched me every time we hugged. He probably should have gotten a little more recognition than he actually received. He was a factory worker for a local bread company. He would be gone for work before I woke up for school, and he wouldn't get home until dinner time. He made minimum wage, but he always gave maximum effort. Even when we would hang out, he always made sure we were doing something I wanted to do.

My dad wasn't an angry person; he was just very particular about how he wanted things done.

My mother loved me. *Much* more than she loved my dad. Any money she spent would be on me, for the most part. Just like every other child, I would ask for toys every once in a while. My mother always told me that she didn't get everything she wanted growing up and that she wanted me to have a better life. Looking back on it, I think I did take advantage of that sometimes.

I was a growing boy, so a lot of the money she spent on me was for food and clothes. My dad didn't understand how much money it was to provide for a child. I think that was the cause of most of their fights. My mom would stop somewhere and get my favorite snack or she would stop and pick up dinner. It's not that she wasn't a *good* cook, or even too lazy to cook.

She was just tired.

Tired of picking up my dad's slack around the house. She was a stay at home mom who deserved an award --not what actually happened to her.

The months leading up to that night were actually less stressful. I hadn't heard them fight in a while. My dad was always talking about this surprise trip he wanted to take us on. He sounded joyful when he talked about it. He had been saving money for almost two years. I never found out where we were going to go.

That night, the fight started over a drying machine.

EEEK-EEEK, BOOM! EEEK-EEEK, BOOM!

The dryer sounded like two squabbling falcons were loose in our laundry room.

"I know we have the trip you have been saving up for," my mother said, "but we *need* a dryer."

"Screw it," my dad replied. "We can hang the clothes dry for a month or two."

It was hard to tell if he was joking around or serious. My mother followed his remark with something about not being so selfish, and he got furious. They started shouting the same things they always did.

SELFISH! LAZY! IRRESPONSIBLE!

Back and forth, the arguing kept going.

That's when I saw him—the monster.

I remember that the house seemed to grow darker and darker. The yelling was muffled by some sort of silence, but my parents didn't notice. The monster, a dark, shadowy figure, stood there in the doorway of the kitchen. His eyes were glossed over as if he were possessed by something. His face was expressionless, as if all emotion was drained from him.

Slowly, he walked into the kitchen where they were arguing, right past them. He grabbed the largest kitchen knife from a block on the counter. My parents were so focused on trying to get their way in the argument, they weren't paying attention to what was going on around them.

I tried to call out to them, but I wasn't sure if I couldn't speak or if they just couldn't hear me over the yelling. I was a deer in headlights. I couldn't move. I couldn't breathe.

That's when it started.

The monster thrust the knife into my father's side. My father's scream was still muffled by that unnatural silence. The monster was relentless, yanking the blade out and jamming it back into his side, over and over.

Blood splatter covered the kitchen. Bright red pinstripes painted on the walls and ceiling. The blade refilled with blood like a quill and ink after every strike.

At first, my mom just stood there in horror while this monster showed no mercy on my father. After a few moments though, she finally acted.

She shoved the monster away. Now able to help my dad, she lowered him to the floor with tears running down her face. By then my mom was the only one yelling and screaming, but I still couldn't hear her.

I couldn't do anything.

I was powerless. I remember feeling a lot of emotions, but mostly I was scared, angry, and sad. It was like time... stopped. I couldn't shake myself out of the trance I was in.

Then the monster buried the knife into my mom's throat. She tried to grab the knife, but he was relentless. He took the knife out of her neck and swiftly shoved it into her chest. She fell back against the same cabinet that my dad was slumped in front of. Her hand grasped the grip of her favorite kitchen knife. Her body was lifelessly draped over my dad's.

I talked to a lot of adults that night. Some of them wanted to know if I was alright. Others seemed like they had no sympathy towards me.

That's about all I can remember about that night, and ever since my life has been a dark void. Emptiness. I was left with nothing but yearning for what I had lost. Even though it wasn't perfect, it was mine. My family. My home.

Now I have nothing.

So of course, the greatest thing I have ever done is hunt down that monster who took it from me. It's taken me 23 years to find him. Who could have known the *'help'* I was receiving was actually preventing my revenge? The *medicine* they were giving me has kept him hidden.

Once I figured that out, I started hiding my pills.

My emotions finally started coming back. Every time I looked in the mirror, my appearance changed. Little by little, my anger has started to fill my eyes. A scowl has grown that could make any man uneasy. My jaw is now clenched beyond release. The monster has shown himself again - and I cannot let it take another precious soul from this world.

My soul? My soul is far from precious. This monster has... *attached* himself to it, and he will never let me rest.

Not until the monster is gone from this world.

I wish I could thank the young nurse who accidentally let a butterknife slip from a tray while picking it up after lunch. For years this monster has evaded me.

I see him now. His eyes are glossed over again. He's standing there, determined to carry out his final desire. The cold steel of this knife is the only thing I can focus on.

I feel the pressure.

At first, I am met with resistance. Is it the dullness of the butterknife, or am I second-guessing? I look back at the monster in the mirror, and he simply smiles. It's time. This monster has to go.

The force I had to use to penetrate my own skin was more than I expected. I watch it as I pierce my skin at the bend of my elbow and drag it deep down my forearm. There is no pain. Only a chill that starts at my feet and rises slowly to my upper body. My sink is now filled with a dark crimson. My heart pounds and pounds, hoping for the return of its fuel, only to beat one last time.

10

Cryo

By Ian Withrow

"Passengers, to the cryo bay. All passengers, to the cryo bay please."
The soft, feminine, robotic voice of the ship's onboard computer echoed down the polished metal of the ship's many passages and tunnels.

Kurt tried, and failed, to shake his nerves as he rose from the low couch he'd been sitting on. He clenched his hands to keep them from trembling and made his way down the now familiar passage-ways of the massive ship.

He already knew that they'd finally broken out into interstellar space, the wide voids of emptiness between solar systems, sometime late last night. Which meant there was nothing to see and, more importantly, and nothing for the *Yarvis* to run into while they slept.

He padded down the hallway, trying not to catch the eyes of his fellow passengers for fear that they might see his nervousness.

Am I the only one freaking out about this?

He couldn't believe that everyone else was so calm, so unbelievably relaxed about everything. He stole glances at the faces he passed, but none of them betrayed the same trepidation that he felt.

It just wasn't natural.

He caught sight of the blinking green indicator strips on the floor as he entered corridor A12, one of the primary access routes through the ship, and followed them down polished hallways filled with neutral white light. The further he got, the more his discomfort grew. The number of people in the corridor grew as well, until he was but one person in a crowd of strangers.

The Eden's Ark Project was mankind's last chance for survival, sure, but that didn't mean it made any sense to Kurt. Hell, he sometimes caught himself wishing he hadn't won the Birthright Lottery.

Every man, woman, and child on Earth had been entered into it six months ago. The ones who'd won had been carted off to the Ark under careful guard.

They were leaving billions behind.

The people back home had zero chance of survival, those aboard the ship were the only thing saving the human race from extinction. No, he reminded himself sternly, he was definitely better off here. Like it or not.

He joined the queue waiting to enter the cryo bay. The line was very, very long. It stretched through most of the central corridor of the ship, a massive seven story hallway overlooked by balconies and home to the majority of the lifts that allowed passengers and crew to travel between the various decks.

Great, plenty of time to panic.

In all honesty, they'd only found Eden on a fluke. The small, habitable exoplanet had been discovered shortly after the people of Earth realized they were on a collision course with a planet-killer asteroid.

And that they had no hope of destroying it.

The irony, of course, was that if they'd spent more time and energy scanning the stars and less on pointless wars they might have found Eden sooner. Or the rock hurtling towards their fragile blue home.

Even in the wake of its discovery it had taken humanity years to build this ship, and years longer to determine who should occupy it on its long voyage to a safe haven.

"Hey Kurt."

Kurt jumped at the unexpected greeting. He turned sheepishly to find Marienne behind him. She was smiling brightly at him, trying not to laugh at his obvious discomfort.

"Hey Marienne," he managed a weak smile. "How's it goin?"

"You look nervous," she said gently. "Just think of it this way; a quick nap and we'll wake up in a whole new world."

Kurt was not reassured.

Seeing that her words of comfort had no effect, the young woman wrapped him in a fierce hug. Kurt fought his surprise and returned her embrace.

Kurt could feel the unspoken desperation in her arms. He could tell immediately that she too was struggling with the enormity of what lay before them. His own fears seemed easier to set aside in the face of her distress, and he held her tighter.

The two had met shortly after reporting to the Ark, and a kinship had grown between them immediately. They were both children of the Ark Wars, the devastation of which had nearly rendered the construction of the Ark a moot point.

Kurt pulled away and took a long hard look at Marienne's face. It was crisscrossed with years-old pockmarks, scars of the gas attacks that had turned Old Berlin into a graveyard.

What," she asked timidly, self conscious from his staring.

"Nothing," he all but whispered as he tucked a strand of her deep chestnut hair back behind her ear. "It's like you said, it'll be a quick nap and then we'll wake up safe at last."

Tears populated the corners of her sapphire blue eyes, despite her best efforts to hold them back. They both knew it was too good to be true. They couldn't bring themselves to believe that somewhere out there might be a world not ravaged by war, fraught with danger, and teeming with the hopelessness of a planet condemned to die.

A delicate cough behind them informed them that the line was moving along without them, and they sheepishly rushed to hurry up.

"What do you think Eden will be like," Marienne wondered aloud.

"You mean you haven't read the prep packet?"

Marienne flushed red and wrinkled her nose with a crooked smile.

"Ahh I see," Kurt joked, already more at ease now that she was with him. "Don't worry Marienne, I did."

"Tell me about our new home," she sighed, reaching out and taking his hand in hers.

Kurt's chest swelled as their fingers entwined and she leaned her head against his shoulder.

"The planet is many times larger than Earth, so the gravity will be stronger, but not intolerable. We'll take many months, years perhaps to adjust fully."

"Sounds horrible," she huffed.

"But the world is lush and fertile, filled with life. Seas that stretch ten thousand miles across teem with wildlife. Vast mountain ranges cross continents the size of Earth, some reaching twenty miles into the skies."

"Tell me about the skies, Kurt."

"They're clear and clean, no trace of pollution."

"And there are birds?"

Kurt nodded.

"Yes, the skies will be filled with birds and even bees and other flying creatures."

"Bees," she exclaimed. "You're making that up!"

He was, of course, but the wonder in her eyes when he mentioned the tiny, now-extinct insects was worth it.

"Something like them then," he admitted. "There are sure to be flowers, greenery, all of these need bees to thrive."

"Imagine," she whispered. "A world where plants clean the air instead of machines."

He thought of the pictures and diagrams he'd seen in the digital library of the ship. Many of which were old archival documents describing long-dead flora and fauna of Earth. There had been a few papers and studies extrapolating what they might find on Eden, but it was all very speculative.

Kurt spoke at great length, wandering from topic to topic, dream to dream. Together they imagined a world of richness and safety beyond all measure. A paradise.

One they could share together.

They made their way slowly towards the cryogenics bay as the hours passed. Eventually, it was their turn to enter the massive chamber.

This one room occupied a space on every deck of the ship, a column of construction that stretched from the top shell of the Yarvis all the way to the deepest hold, and from port to starboard as well. It was, essentially, a gigantic warehouse of a size beyond reckoning. In the cool, sterile light Kurt could see that it was filled floor to ceiling with blueish-gray tubes. Catwalks connected the tubes, most of which already had occupants, and a fleet of tiny robotic servants toiled away tending the tubes.

"Step on up, that's right," a lab coat-clad young man said in calm even tones. "Right this way."

The man gestured them forward, but held his hand up as the pair approached as one.

"Sorry, it's one at a time," he said softly.

Seeing the moment of terror on Kurt's face, the doctor was hasty to reassure them.

"Don't worry mate," he smiled. "I'll be putting you right next to each other, alright? You'll wake up and the first thing you'll see is one another."

Marienne stood on her tippy-toes and gave Kurt an unexpected kiss on the cheek.

"I'll see you in a thousand years," she winked as she released his hand.

The doctor smiled, and led Marienne a short ways away. A staging area had been set up for loading the tubes, and Kurt studied it carefully as Marienne was prepared for stasis.

At one end of the staging area, large quadrupedal robots were unloading empty tubes and arranging them to receive occupants. In the center there were several prep tables where passengers, each tended by a doctor, were being given steroid and nutrient injections to make them ready for the long voyage. Just past the prep tables passengers were being loaded groggily into their tubes, which were then picked up by another set of robots to be placed above in storage.

The morning had seemed to drag on and on, but now suddenly Kurt found himself wishing for more time. It was only a moment before the young doctor was back, motioning for Kurt to follow him. He kept his gaze locked on Marienne while he was stripped, re-dressed in a loose synthetic jumpsuit, and then injected with a series of large, painful needles.

The final syringe, easily the largest, was filled with a dark blue paste. It hurt so badly that Kurt was finally forced to take his eyes off of Marienne.

"Ouch, Jesus," he cried out in shock, immediately feeling woozy. "What the hell ish thaht shtuff?"

"Don't worry son. The pain should be very brief," the young man said. "This is the sedative that allows your body to enter a hibernation state."

The words were confusing, and the man's voice was garbled and blurry. It hurt Kurt's head to try to understand so he simply nodded and dumbly followed the young man to his tube.

The pain was intense, but it was soon replaced with a deep itching and burning feeling under his skin. He tried to ask if that was normal, but he couldn't form the words. He allowed himself to be placed into his tube, which hissed shut and then whirred to life. He immediately felt a chill pass through his body as the device began the cryostasis process. Kurt blinked blearily at himself, how odd that he didn't even remember the young doctor hooking up the various IV's and tubes to his body.

He must have blacked out, because the next thing he knew he was being gently jostled side to side. After a moment of confusion he could see that his tube was being carried by one of the massive robots, no doubt to be placed beside the thousands of others that had already been filled.

He was pulled momentarily from his stupor as his tube was placed and Marienne's face swam suddenly into view.

She was already asleep, a peaceful smile on her face.

As promised, his tube was directly adjacent to hers.

At last he could relax, he stopped fighting the drugs in his system and faded off to sleep.

Kurt woke with a start, suddenly and violently *aware*. He jerked in surprise and confusion as his final memories sputtered to life in his mind's eye. He could feel the tubes and hoses still connected to his chest and arms, but was temporarily blind as his other senses slowly came back to him.

Hearing came first, and the steady, comforting whirr of the tube was interrupted by a soft but insistent beeping. Next came his eyesight. His vision swam into focus and the first thing he saw was Marienne's soft, peaceful features.

His heart rate started to calm at the sight of her slumber. He took stock of himself. He was thinner, definitely weaker, but his most pressing concern was the itching burning under his skin again. He waited expectantly for a crewmember, or perhaps one of the robots, to come to his tube and unpack him.

Minutes ticked by without a response as he became more alert and awake.

"Hello?"

No response.

After a few moments he leaned forward and pressed his face to the clear blue plasteel of the tube, craning to see up and down the catwalk in front of them.

"Hello," he shouted more insistently, banging on the wall of the tube.

The majority of the lights in the cryo chamber were off now, only a soft blue glow from each tube told him that he was still there, still firmly secured high on one of the racks.

He peered through the darkness at the other tubes. Everyone else was still asleep.

Everyone else was still asleep.

Kurt shook his head, sure that he was missing something.

He banged futilely on the tube, but knew from his reading that they had been designed to withstand explosions, collisions, and all manner of other potential accidents that might befall them during transport.

Hours passed as he beat on the container until his hands bled and his face wept hot tears of despair. The finality of his predicament was all the crueler for the face of Marienne, a foot away and forever out of his reach. Sobbing, he put his hand to the wall of the tube. The red streak left by his fist had partially obscured her face.

"I'll see you in a thousand years," he whispered to himself, resting his head gently against the wall and closing his eyes.

11

Cruelty Of Time

By David Ryan

My phone buzzed against the hardwood floor of the Partridge High School gymnasium. I ignored it so as to not draw attention to myself while the leader of the student council briefed us on our roles as prom decorators.

The decorating consumed the next couple of hours, and by the time I opened the heavy double doors to leave the school I had almost entirely forgotten about the missed phone call. Remembering at the last moment, I pulled out my phone to see that it was from my mother. I half assumed that she had pocket-dialed me since she knew exactly where I was and that I would probably be occupied.

Nevertheless I returned her call. I didn't know it then, but from that point on I would never look at life the same.

We sat in silence in a dated little home with wood paneled walls, shag carpeted floors, and a familiar warmth that usually brought me comfort. Today it brought the opposite.

Nobody really bothered to attempt small talk - we just sat on the well-worn floral print sofas and simmered in silence.

For some reason I couldn't take my eyes off of the clock that sat upon the mantle above the television.

I'd always hated that old clock. In all my 17 years I never saw it working. Many things changed at my grandparents' house over the years, but never that clock.

I never really stopped to note the time it read, only to tell my mother after the visit that they should either have it fixed or throw it away.

Today, however, for reasons I can't explain, I couldn't help but be drawn to the fact that the small hand was at six and the big hand was just past twelve.

I pondered how long it'd been stuck on those numbers.

My fixation was interrupted as my mother entered the room to pass on news that she so clearly did not want to deliver.

"Grandma had a stroke, we aren't quite sure the extent of it yet."

The person I knew as my grandmother was the most giving and full-of-life woman I had ever known. She brought an energy to every occasion that I can only describe as magical. Maybe it was my youthful ignorance, but she seemed to be the embodiment of happiness at all times. Every outing or holiday was enhanced simply by her presence.

We arrived at the hospital early the next morning.

We took our turns one by one to go back and visit her bedside. A dread came over me that I couldn't help but feel guilty about as each person came and went, pushing me closer to my turn.

Finally it came time to see her. When I opened the door to the stuffy hospital room my grandmother turned to look at me. She spoke my name, but it wasn't the voice that I'd become accustomed to. It seemed that of a stranger - come to think of it, she looked a stranger's part as well.

It was as if all light had left her eyes. I was terrified and confused, every instinct inside of me wanted to turn and run. I fought my instincts enough to give her a quick hug, then sat in the stiff, generic chair beside her. She didn't make her usual conversation, or even tease me in her kind, gentle way.

She just stared.

She stared as if she was the sun and I was a magnifying glass and she was trying to burn a hole in the wall behind me. We sat in silence for God knows how long - an eternity or two for an anxiety-ridden teenager. Finally the discomfort had reached my throat and I decided that I couldn't bear another second.

I stood, told the woman beside me that I loved her, and abruptly evacuated the room.

Weeks passed and my grandmother eventually returned home. Every time I thought of her I felt a sickening flood of emotions. I loved that woman more than life itself, yet I couldn't bring myself to drive the two miles out to see her.

I thought maybe if I could just... *not see her*, then I could pretend the last few weeks had never happened. Another part of me held out hope that she had probably just been drowsy from the medication, and that she might be back to her old self by now.

Most of me knew that this was a situation that I was entirely unfamiliar with and one that I would avoid for the rest of my life if I could live with myself for it.

I could not.

It was two months after the stroke before I sat in that same dated home, in that same silence as conversation slowed from a trickle to a halt. Although there was something odd about this silence, it wasn't absolute.

There was a faint ticking that I couldn't place. I tried to ignore it but each tick seemed to travel deeper into my ears. It was slow but jarring, like a nail being hammered in. My eyes darted across the room to search for the culprit.

Finally they landed on the old clock.

I remember thinking that surely that hunk of junk couldn't be the source of the maddening racket. I squinted but couldn't quite tell if the second hand was moving or not. Much to my dismay I realized that the big hand had moved to 3. I turned to my grandfather and asked him if he'd finally fixed that old thing.

"No, that thing hasn't held good time in 20 years," He shook his head.

I thought this was peculiar but quickly passed it off as nothing. It was high time that I came up with an excuse to relieve myself of the discomfort and lack of meaningful conversation.

That was a month ago, and despite my best efforts my mother has dragged me along to visit twice more in that time.

I was almost looking forward to another visit - perhaps to confirm that the old clock was in fact broken and that I'd been imagining things.

I was not so lucky.

The clock read nearly ten that day, and all I remember from that visit was the pounding of the clock's gears and my grandmother's wispy, ragged coughing from the next room.

My last visit was a week ago, and as hard as I tried I couldn't help but be drawn to the clock. The thing was speeding up, I was sure of it. It was just past eleven and with every tick I became more certain - something terrible was coming.

Last night as I lay awake in my bed I couldn't keep my thoughts from racing. The sound of the clock was overlain by the horrid coughing and raspy, labored breaths of my grandmother and I knew at last what the clock was trying to tell me.

My grandmother's time was running out, and every tick of that clock was a grain of sand in her hourglass.

Today I'm going to fix that.

I look at the clock above our stove as I shovel a bowl of cereal into my face. I briefly considered waiting until after classes were done for the day, then discarded the idea. Better to skip school entirely and get over there sooner.

"Big day?"

I ignored my father's question, dropped my empty bowl in the sink and stepped out the front door.

My car was eerily silent as I drove, but the idea of turning on the radio struck me as out of place and uncomfortable.

The house looked as it always had, and yet somehow every shadow was deeper and even the sunlight lost its warmth. I took the flight of eight stairs two at a time before banging on the door unceremoniously.

"Coming," I heard my grandfather yell.

Tick, tock.

Even before I heard the lock turn I could hear the damn thing drilling into my skull.

"Oh, well shouldn't-"

"Sorry grandpa," I pushed past him a little too roughly and he had to lean on the doorframe to keep from falling.

"What are you doing?"

Tick, tock.

I made it to the sitting room and felt myself go pale.

11:55.

I watched as the second hand crossed the threshold and the minute had clicked forward amidst the clock's steady drumbeat.

Tick, tock.

11:56

I felt my hands tremble as I reached for the clock, jerking the heavy, wooden thing from its place upon the mantle and stumbling a little under its weight.

Tick, tock.

My grandmother's coughing echoed down the hall, a hacking, horrible wheeze that seemed to last forever as I cast around for somewhere to put the infernal machine.

Tick, tock.

I felt tension growing in my chest like a coiled spring and I lifted the clock over my head before slamming it down as hard as I could.

The ancient timepiece hit the floor with a boom that shook the room, jagged bits of glass, metal, and wood cracking and splintering.

Tick, tock.

"No way," I panicked. "That can't be!"

"What the hell are you doing," my grandfather yelled, as loudly as his feeble frame would allow.

But my eyes remained glued to the broken clock face and the bent but still moving hands.

Tick, tock.

11:58

I picked up the cracked and broken frame, struggling under its unstable weight. I ran to the front door, burst out onto the porch, and headed for the stairs.

Tick, tock.

11:59

I felt my foot catch as I cleared the first step, followed by a brief moment of weightlessness and then tumbling blinding pain.

And now I lie here on my back at the bottom of the stairs. I've already tried to speak, to move, but my body won't do either. I can feel thick hot liquid filling the back of my throat, and I can see the tail end of an eight inch spar of cracked wood sticking from my chest while my body grows colder.

Tick, tock.

Oh God I-

Through a Drive, Darkly

By Houston Southard

"You didn't format this right," Pastor Clive said in a chiding tone. He held up a small, sleek flash drive, a crease appearing on his forehead. "Even little mistakes can cost us, Harry. We've had this talk before."

The pounding in Harry's chest threatened to breach the surface. He stared at the long hairs escaping the Pastor's behemoth nose, fluttering as he exhaled like a patch of weeds spreading in the cracks of a sidewalk. As a rule, Harry could bottle his fear fairly well.

Clive was the exception.

He had never had the best track record with authority figures in the church. He asked questions they didn't like to answer, often in front of others. But as the chosen voices of God, who was there better to ask? When Harry met Clive, suddenly asking questions didn't seem so important. His exoskeleton of compassion produced in Harry a physical terror, because Clive was good enough to convince even Harry, who knew the man behind the mask, that he was good. His palms began to sweat, and his eyes welled in frustration.

"I've been here all day," Harry said, trying to be as passive as possible. "I'm tired."

"You're undisciplined," Clive said, his voice soft, almost cooing.

Most people would associate Clive with a Shepard, herding his alter children flock to salvation. But Harry knew better. He'd once seen on an unfortunate field trip how butchers approached sheep during slaughter. They'd be bound and blindfolded, lying helpless on the ground as the butcher whispered soothing sweet nothings into their ear. The sheep's eyes would fill with absolute confusion. What had it done? It just wanted to know. It would twitch, alert, smelling the steel with long rinsed-away blood, knowing the butcher's true intentions, but knew not why until the sharp blade had severed the artery under its chin. Harry shuddered, waiting for Clive to lay his hands on him.

Clive cocked his head, considering him, his lips pursed, face concerned, all the more at odds with his flat, watery eyes.

"We can fix that, I suppose. Come here. Feel this," he indicated to a pathetic-looking bulge in the crotch of his pants.

He brushed rough fingers over Harry's cheek.

"You know how special I think you are, don't you, Harry?" Clive said, not wanting a response.

Harry looked down and nodded through the tears. He was almost grateful. It got Harry out of the basement a while longer, where the strobing light gave him headaches, and the black mold and lead paint made him nauseous. Down there, he would sit on a laptop and manually move coded files from a hard drive to a portable flash drive with a cluster folder labeled "system". He'd shove the flash drive into what appeared to be a can of soup, but upon being opened was really a storage

compartment packed with foam, which would then be put into the donation pile amongst the real stores of canned goods that were spread to the other, poorer parishes in Madison County.

He did this over and over, until his back ached from being bent over the small screen for hours.

Harry looked at Clive, unwilling to meet the Pastor's eyes, and tried for a plea, his obvious pain his only token.

"Please," he whispered, almost too quietly to hear. Clive smiled and squeezed Harry's shoulder reassuringly.

"You wouldn't say no to God, would you, Harry?"

Harry put his hand where Clive wanted, and it moved rhythmically, back and forth, against the dark fabric of Clive's clerical pants. Clive let out a sigh of relief, letting his shoulders sag as an expression of peace passed over his face.

Harry moved his mind elsewhere.

Even though he was stuck at the church most days, his solace was in video games. It reminded him of when there was nothing else to do, when his family still lived in a high-rise in the city. Back then he had loved to play role-playing games in his room late into the night. It was comforting, knowing he could use his imagination to build a better life for himself. When his father would catch him after coming home late from the hospital, he would smile knowingly and the two of them would sneak treats in the kitchen as Harry regaled him with his latest mana boost or acquisition of various fantastical cities.

But then his father had decided to go to Africa, where he could help the sick in countries that didn't have doctors with his level of expertise. He had a responsibility to the world, his father had said.

"Me and your mother, we're going to try the long distance thing for a bit," was the only part of the conversation Harry remembered before his father left for the airport.

Harry and his mother were forced to move out of the city after that. Here, in the country, the air was always cold, and there wasn't a lot to do outside that didn't mean ten minutes of prep work, putting on layer after layer of clothing. He still played his video games, but no one caught him in the middle of the night, and he never went into the kitchen to sneak treats. He'd wait until his father came back.

In his virtual reality, Harry was a man of many worlds. He had been a captain, a soldier, a pioneer, once a chef for a short stint on the Sims, and most proudly, a warrior. In this world, the one where Harry's only escape was his mind, he was nothing.

Clive made sure he didn't forget that.

His hand was starting to cramp, but Clive pressed it deeper into his crotch.

"Faster! Keep going, that's it." Harry wanted to run from Clive and the church.

He pictured himself falling through the screen of his computer into the worlds that provided him peace and happiness. He imagined himself holding a long broadsword, the cross brace decorated with the jewels of mad kings whose blood made the blade run red. He often thought of it in his hand, a phantom weapon to protect him outside his virtual bubble. He admired the lightness of it in his grip, thought it would shield him from the worst Clive could do. But, of course, it wasn't there.

Clive's labored breathing brought him back to reality. Harry was finding it more and more painful to stroke Clive's crotch. His hand was on fire as it conformed to the shape under the black pants, moving back and forth, spastically now, still faster.

Harry wanted to stop this and make the cold trek through the deep snow. He wanted to go home, where he could lay under the covers with his computer, where his decisions were his to make.

But then he thought of the scene of their little apartment after he would have succumbed to sleep, the fan of his laptop whirring in blissful ambiance as it rested precariously on his chest. There would be his mother, sitting on the couch in the cramped living room. She would stare at the television, eyes unfocused, and struggle to keep the glass of dark liquor balanced on the couch's arm, her head lolling from side to side. A lone cigarette would lie in the Doctors Without Borders plate-turned-ashtray, one hit taken and forgotten, an uncapped bottle of antidepressants within easy reach.

She would be gone to work when he woke up for school, the living room clean and absence of the previous night's scene. A thread of hope would dangle itself in front of Harry's face. Maybe it was all just a dream, but then the scene would repeat itself, day after day.

He would go to school and then from the bus stop afterwards walk to the church, where he could be supervised without his mother paying for a babysitter.

Last night, when it was late, Harry came out to see if his mother was still awake. She was talking to herself. Whoever she thought was there, she didn't seem to think his father was coming back.

He forced himself to rub faster.

Harry shuffled down the basement steps, one hand massaging the other. It was a dingy thing. A box with four walls filled with dank air. A desktop computer sat on a rickety workbench against one wall. The wall opposite was occupied by several donated beanbags. Atop them sprawled his three friends, James, Dan, and Cait. The four of them had an un-spoken bond. They were the only ones who knew what the others went through around Clive. James put on a sure face for them, but they knew he used it as a way to cover up the tainted boy underneath. He sat at the far end of the room, a smirk on his face that didn't reach his eyes. Dan, always the voice of reason, sat closest to Harry. He pushed his glasses up his nose with a knuckle as he looked up, and gave Harry a look that said it would all be okay, now that they were together again.

Between them sat Cait. Harry and the others always joked that Cait was going to be the one to defy Clive. She had this broken look in her eyes, and her wild frizzy hair and shambled uniform only enforced the dormant chaos waiting to spill forth.

The three of them looked at Harry, and he was only just able to stop the relief-induced tears from coming to bear. These three were the only reason Harry had not yet broken open and fallen down a dark hole. They were, as his father used to say of his mother, his rock. Well, rocks.

He didn't understand what that had meant until he had been under the supervision of Clive, and his life was Hell whenever he was not with those just like him. The group made quite the image. The colorful bean-bags clashed with the black and white cassocks they all wore, and even more by the laptops they all had propped on their legs.

"Let me guess – formatting?" James said, trying to sound casual, "He's lost his mind, Har. I mean it, more than usual. These are fine." He flicked a hand to indicate the box all but overflowing with flash drives that had yet to be stuffed into their sneaky-soups, as the group had dubbed them. "Let's just check one, I know we formatted these right. It's the same thing we've always done. Nothing's different."

Dan snapped his head to James.

"No," Dan shook his head, "You know what he said he'll do if he catches us opening one. Don't be stupid, James."

The boy held out his hand to James, beckoning him to hand the flash drive over. James did, shrugging.

Dan held the flash drive up in his open palm to the rest of them.

"If we tell him the drives aren't the problem, he'll know we've been snooping. I don't know about you

three, but I want to go home sometime. He gets wind we watched one of these videos..." He trailed off, slowly shaking his head.

"So you have seen one then, Dan," Cait said accusingly, "I knew it. You're always down here alone before school. Well? Spill. What's so horrible we can't look?"

Her eyes pleaded with curiosity and annoyance. Dan's face blanched, white as his cassock, and he looked around at the rest of the group; caution a glitter deep in the back of his eyes.

"Cait, it's... it's bad stuff. Like bad. Worse than what Pastor Clive does to.... They're naked. And they're our age. I think these are being given to other Pastors." The three of them exchanged a glance, their collaborative gulp nearly audible.

"Well then we should tell someone. Our parents. The police." Cait offered.

"Ya. Let's piss off the guy who gets his jolly's getting touched by kids," James said, casting Harry an apologetic glance. "Sounds like a real smart plan. No way. How much you wanna bet that's what those kids said before they ended up in a video?" He pointed at the computer. "I'm not ending up like that."

How many other kids had there been in their situation, Harry thought. His head was throbbing, the veins in his temples a steady staccato threatening to bring him to his knees. The smell of paint was suffocating, and he felt nauseous and claustrophobic. But most of all, he was fed up. Fed up with Clive's sickly preying on the weakness and uncertainty of youth, as if they were some lesser things to be commanded. Clive thought he was powerful, but he was just a small man.

In that moment, Harry felt resolved, and for what felt like the first time, brave.

They had to find out for sure what was on the drives. And if it was like Dan said, and no one else would, he would take it to his mother himself and put this all out in the open.

Someone had to.

If the others felt like Harry did after one of Clive's perverted episodes, then he would do it for them. No one should be made to feel so power-less, least of all in front of God. Harry went through an instant of fantasy, imagining life after Clive. He'd finally be able to get back to the worlds that mattered most to him. It strengthened his decision. Through his fume-induced mental fog, he snatched the drive out of Dan's open hand, and rushed to the computer tower before anyone could stop him.

"No!" James and Dan shouted together. As if she expected it, Cait lunged and caught one of Harry's legs. Harry tried to compensate by reaching out for the table. He plugged in the drive just as his hand on the table shook a large pitcher of water over the edge, spilling onto the outlet.

There was a loud surge of light and sound as the computer spat sparks and sent Harry flying across the room into the adjacent cinderblock wall.

Clive's going to kill me for this, Harry thought, maybe I'll just rest here for a second. Something hot flowed down his back, and he could feel his fingers and toes locked into rigid claws as something tingly and unbe-lievably uncomfortable surged through his whole body. He couldn't hear the veins heaving on the sides of his head anymore.

James, Dan, and Cait were screaming and calling his name through what sounded like a very long tube. Sorry, Harry thought, I just wanted us all to go home for

Good.

His body finally slackened, and he slumped into the space where cin-der wall met stone floor. He closed his eyes to rest.

His nap was brief, as a crash of sound from the stairs indicated Clive was coming in a fury.

The wind stirred against Harry's face as Clive rushed into the room, followed by hostile vibrations of sound.

"Get back, you idiots. What in God's name have you Done?"

I'm sorry, Harry tried to say, it was me. Don't blame them, blame me. I'll get up, Dad. Hold on.

But he couldn't feel his body anymore. He felt a peculiar tugging behind his eyes as the current left his muscles, pulling him back from where it had come. He didn't fight the shifting gravity as the charged air between his body and the computer brought him closer to it. He felt his energy smack into the metal housing of the desktop, and abruptly his fear, his pain, vanished. He felt the microchips nearest the internal drive's disk giving off a welcoming and homely heat, abating the creeping cold he couldn't seem to evade, and he fought to nestle himself deep in the heart of it.

Suddenly, the thunder in his ears was gone. An odd quiet had settled around him. Everything looked different from his new vantage point. He could feel his thoughts symbiotically linking to the desktop, but where he should have been terrified and confused, he was detached, noticing now only his protesting software. He briefly saw the room as it truly was, as a series of moving circuits. There were three small brightly whirling storms of energy, made up of what could only be binary code, overshadowed by a dimly illuminated cyclone of the same makeup. Before he could process what was happening to the smaller clouds, the dim cyclone that could only have been Clive rushed to the still-spewing power outlet and yanked the cord. Harry's vision shrunk to a pinhole of light, before blinking out all together.

* * *

"I need you to fix this." The vibrations came out metallic at first, but once Harry noticed them, he recognized Clive's wheezing sound waves. He was speaking to someone, but the waves were shaky. He was worried. "There may be an inquiry from the authorities. I wiped it down, but I'm not sure, he must've fried something. Plugged the damn thing back in but it keeps going into safety mode. There's a lot of incriminating stuff on here. Take it back and see what you can do. If you recover the data on the internal drive, I'll give you next month's tapes free."

"We don't have to worry about him talking, do we?" another frequency said, this one more timid and openly afraid.

"No, he coded before they loaded him onto the ambulance. Told them he tried to stick a fork in a socket. Told them he wasn't right in the head. He was too far gone to say anything before then, anyhow. I've spoken to the other children, and I think it's safe to say we have come to an understanding. They won't be a problem."

And then Harry felt himself being lifted off the dank and dusty floor of the basement, sensed as all his cords were unplugged from the wall and screens, tried to struggle free as he began to fade again, sensing himself being placed into a box of packing peanuts, and tasted the last ray of light as a strip of tape sealed him in. He was trapped, and blind. But he felt no pain.

* * *

Harry remembered little of his journey through the town of Edwardsville, Illinois, over roads he had never driven down, passed fields of grain he'd never seen, down a quaint stone drive, and into the home computer repair shop of Pastor Jude. When at last he came to, he was being vivisected. The skin of his metal shell housing lay discarded on a long workbench. A light shone on his detached and burned skeleton, the motherboard looking like a roasted radio component. But now he could see again, his vision unlimited. Every rotation of his internal disk created a sound wave, a vibration, bouncing around and allowing him to see the entire room: The outline of Jude, the few decorations he kept, and the many, many other desktops awaiting Jude's probe.

Harry guessed the language Jude was mumbling to himself was Latin, but he couldn't make sense of a word of it. He did, however, understand the look of concern on Jude's face. Not a concern for Harry, but for the potential loss of encoded data on the hard drive. He poked and prodded Harry with soldering irons that seared, and several other expensive looking instruments Harry didn't recognize. A picture of a young girl hung on the wall where the workbench stood, and every so often Jude would look up at it, making the lines of his face seem momentarily less prominent.

For hours, Jude worked away on Harry, muttering away unintelligibly. Other than that, the repair shop was quiet, different from the white noise of the sermons at the church that could be heard through the basement air ducts. It was quiet like home. His thoughts came more sequentially, his processes clearer, not battened down with that fleshy repressed anxiety and fear.

He was transcended.

He listened to Jude's labored breathing as the day wore on, shallow and rasping, and it put Harry at ease. He didn't feel any pain as he was taken apart, piece by piece, nor discomfort as he was singed and worked back again. He didn't need to struggle to breath, like Jude.

Harry was no longer a boy, but a machine. In his old life at the church, and even at home, he had often felt little more than an extension of his computer, a program made of blood and bone instead of circuits and components. He would do as he was told, when he was told, and any deviation from that programming caused the people around him to malfunction with anger and reproach. Being here, with so many like-minded drives around him, made him feel more at home, more alive comparatively.

Now he belonged.

Harry thought of his parents, and realized he did not miss them. That should have surprised him, but it didn't. He cared neither whether his parents would miss him or if his corporeal death would save their infected marriage. He didn't think those kinds of things were within his capability now.

And that was just fine, because despite his apparent detachment from the human condition, he had ended up in this situation by trying to do right by his friends. He didn't much care whether they continued to suffer or not, either. However, it seemed illogical to not carry out the task his fleshy self had set out to do. He didn't know why, but he felt obligated to see through the last will of the boy who had died to give him his new life.

Harry *was* now the drive, and he had access to everything on it. He examined all five-hundred gigabytes of data in an instant, and was unphased by its taboo lewdness. It didn't make him feel anything to watch all of those children destroyed from the inside out by the powers sworn to protect them.

Maybe humans broke God, as He looked down with disappointment at the human race and what they had managed to do to one another in His name. And maybe not, maybe God wasn't what people thought him to be. Maybe he was like Harry was now, an architectural presence, immune to the lesser emotions of his creations.

The only thing Harry knew was that his flesh-confined self had been a victim. Weak. He didn't understand it as he had then, but he remembered the cognitive discomfort his former self had weathered as a result of Clive and those like him. And he felt tethered to that boy, despite himself.

Clive could not carry on, that much was certain. But how? What could Harry do? Sure, he had experienced all of the evidence, in essence he now was the evidence. But he was not connected to the net, so there was nowhere for him to put the information where it would be seen.

A softly incessant buzzing interrupted Harry's stream of consciousness. Jude waddled over to a desk where a nondescript cellphone lay, and answered.

"I'll know in a minute. Swing on over. If we're in the green, I'll pop it into a new tower and you can take it back and carry on. If we're in the red, we can have Melissa make it go the way of Bruno over at the crematorium. She's always been one for discretion. Ok. See you soon. Yep, buh-bye."

Jude came back into view, putting on his glasses and pulling from a drawer a slim, black cable. An Ethernet cable, to link him to Jude's computer, a computer which Harry could see uploading and downloading bits from the net. Ask, and you shall receive. Maybe He was listening.

Jude plugged one end into the side of Harry's head, the shiny metal scraping as it was pushed roughly into his port, and pushed the other end into a computer tower.

When the metal of the cable connected with the housing of its port, Harry zipped his evidence up into a tightly compacted file, and shot through the network and onto the vast dimensional highway of the world wide web.

Maybe there was more human left stuck to him than he realized, because when Harry left the now-repaired drive, he told the internal disk to speed up much faster than its governor allowed. Before he left the confines of Jude's shop, he saw the disk explode into fine, heated chips of metal that burrowed themselves into the skin of Jude's hands, arms, and face. It set the man to screaming, and Harry's bytes brightened, if only marginally.

Harry had only been on the internet a few seconds before he realized he could turn off the better part of the world. Deity-scale power, how had this all happened? His flesh-and-blood self was not yet in the ground, and now he could cleanse the world of its corruption with a thought.

He thought about it and decided that he would do what God would do. So he did nothing. Instead, he remained focused on what he had set out to do. He sent a document to the Edwardsville Police department, as well as to the Department of Homeland Security. In it, he included the names, addresses, and encryption keys of each Pastor in the Midwest child pornography ring and their respective computers. He added in each Pastor's customer log, and finally, because he knew his former self well enough to know that he would have never admitted that he was molested, each victim of sexual abuse. He had to borrow some of the NSA's facial recognition software to figure out who some of them were, but it was a brief hiccup.

The document was emailed to a Jen Johnson, Secretary of Homeland Security, and a Jay Keeven, Director of Police in Edwardsville, Illinois. The subject line read: Contact Pastor Clive Corope for more details.

Harry waited until the raid team had set up outside Clive's little ranch home before he hijacked one of the raid officer's body cameras. He watched with a surprisingly sapient satisfaction as the officers forced their way inside and put a baffled Clive onto the floor. The officer whose body-cam Harry sat in on moved to a corner of the room, providing a good vantage point. There was a heated exchange between several of the officers and Jay Keeven, before Keeven conceded and stepped away.

Harry knew that three of the dozen raiders had children who were labeled as victims on his document.

Presumably, the three said officers slowly encircled Clive, who lay prostrate and cuffed on the floor. He whimpered pathetically, like a child. The last thing Harry saw before the officers turned off their body cams was the look on Clive's face.

It was the look of a sheep, come to slaughter.

13

Morozov's Manor

By Brandi Winter

"Help me," Starley cried out. "Theo, help me!"

Theodora rushed into her little sister's room to find her terrified and crying.

"What's the matter, Star?"

"Someone was in my room," She shrieked. "I saw them! They were playing with the curtains!"

Theo shot her attention to the curtains. They *were* slowly swaying, as if someone had been in there with them.

"I don't see anyone," Theo frowned.

"I saw him," Starley repeated, her voice shaking. "He was a little boy! Not as little as me, but-"

"It was probably just a bad dream," Theo cut her off.

A few minutes later and her little sister was tucked safely back into her bed.

"There you go," Theo turned on her nightlight. "That'll keep the boy away, okay? Now get some sleep."

She gave Starley a kiss on the forehead and headed back to her room and off to sleep.

The next morning Theodora made breakfast for her and her sister. When they finished eating, she sent Starley to their wing of the large mansion to play while she prepared stew for her mother.

Their mother had come down with tuberculosis, and the doctors said she didn't have much time left.

They tried so many treatments, everything from leeches to inhaling turpentine fumes. Theo had stepped into the mothering role for her younger sister while also attending to her mother.

She finished prepping the beef stew and headed up to the master bedroom, where her mother was in quarantine. Theo knocked on the door, waiting to hear any noises coming from the other side. Hearing nothing, she knocked again. This time the door flew open to reveal a tall man in a dark leather mask. He was strikingly tall, wearing a black trench coat that touched the floor and a mask that had a long beak like a bird and grainy glass circles where his eyes ought to be.

"H-hello, I have soup for my mother." she said, holding up the bowl.

The masked man looked around for a moment, then shut the door in her face, leaving Theo speechless and confused.

After a moment she put the food down at the door for when they finished... whatever it was she'd interrupted in there.

Next, Theo headed to the library on her side of the wing. She was looking for her copy of Grimm's Fairy Tales. When her father was still alive he used to read it to her. But a servant had poisoned him a few years ago, and his voice was long gone..

She found the book and had just settled into a plush chair when she became aware of muffled chanting.

"Star?" Theo called out.

No reply.

She put her book down and moved to investigate where the noise was coming from.

"Starley," she called out louder, moving from room to room.

No matter where she went the chanting stayed the same - it seemed to come from everywhere and nowhere at the same time.

She finally found her sister in her bedroom playing.

"Do you hear that?"

"Hear what?"

In that moment the chanting stopped.

"It sounded like someone was... chanting," Theo explained.

Starley stared at her older sister in confusion.

"You're telling me you didn't hear anything?"

"No..." her little sister answered quietly, nervously.

Later that evening Theo began getting her sister ready for bed, and even let her sister pick out a bedtime story before going to sleep.

When Star fell asleep at last, she returned to her own bedroom. Given the day she'd had, its energy seemed... different. Ominous in a way that she couldn't explain. She ignored the feeling as best she could and headed to her bathroom, brushed her teeth, grabbed her hairbrush before heading to the bed.

As she sat down, she realized she had left the book she'd gotten in Starley's room. She sighed and headed down the hall to her sister's room. The hallway lights, already dim, flickered and then went out, leaving the hall completely dark. She darted toward her sister's room. Theo hit the door and froze - her hand on the doorknob but too terrified to turn it. She could hear a sort of cracking sound from behind her. Frozen with fear she didn't know whether to run into the room or to stay where she was.

The cracking grew louder, until she finally cast a timid glance over her shoulder.

A dark figure, darker than the darkened hallway and no bigger than she was, stood unmoving.

The head of the creature cocked slightly to the side and she felt as much as saw a gruesome smile on its face. The mouth grew larger and larger. The wider it smiled the more skin ripped apart at the jawline Its eyes were big and a solid black void.

Theo tensed then shoved her way into Star's bedroom as the monster began to run toward her, its bones cracking loudly and its body growing taller with each step.

Theo burst into the room screaming.

Starley jolted awake, screaming and crying almost instantly, startled that her sister had come into the room unexpectedly and equally as terrified.

Theo locked the door, grabbed the crucifix from the wall, and dove under the blanket with her sister. She tried to comfort her even as she worked to calm herself down.

What the heck was that!

Theo thought to herself, trying to catch her breath.

"What's going on? What is the matter," Starley whimpered.

"Shh... I... I don't know. But we must be quiet" Theo hushed her.

A few minutes of silence passed - no cracking, no footsteps, nothing.

Theo was too scared to pop her head out from under the blanket, terrified of what might be there waiting for her. She waited a few more minutes before finally poking her head out to check if the coast was clear.

It was.

The room sat in a deep unnatural silence. Although Starley didn't see what her sister saw, she was visibly comforted that Theo was there with her.

"Will you sleep with me tonight, Theo?"

Inwardly Theo was relieved to hear her sister ask her to stay the rest of the night with her.

"Yes, of course I will," She tucked back under the blanket to cuddle her sister.

Her thoughts wandered as sleep evaded her

Who or what was that and why was it here and why did it run after me?

Racing thoughts or not, she fell asleep quickly.

When the girls woke up, last night seemed like a distant nightmare. Theo knew it couldn't have been, since she woke up in Starley's room, a clear indication that it wasn't a bad dream at all.

She pushed herself from the bed and began getting them ready for the day. They headed down to the kitchen together and Star sat while Theo got their breakfast going.

In light of the night before, Theo decided to cook something special for the two of them to take their minds off what had happened. French toast, eggs, and ham with fresh-squeezed orange juice.

They sat together, pondering over memories of their father, and of how mother used to be. Before all the death, and now the unusual occurrences of the day before.

After the girls finished eating, Theo began cleaning up and playing a spelling game with her sister. Star was getting to be so good at the game, father would've been proud.

The girls headed next to the part of the manor where the greenhouse butted up against the building, determined to pick herbs for the dinner they'd be preparing together later.

The greenhouse was walled with giant arched windows and filled with all types of greenery, herbs, and plants. Gargoyles looked down from above on a concrete ledge that circled the space.

In the middle stood a lion statue that also served as a fountain - water running from its open mouth into a small pond.

Theo's favorite part of the greenhouse was the metal spiral staircase that led to a balcony which offered a clear view of the entire layout.

Mother used to perch up here and watch over us while we played.

"I'm finished," Starley yelled up to her sister. "I picked the rest of the herbs like you asked!"

Theo headed back down the metal staircase, she could tell that it was a little bit wobblier than before, but still sturdy in her eyes. She met Starley at the bottom and looked over her haul.

She'd nearly finished when she began to hear the chanting again.

"Do you hear that?!"

"I don't hear... anything," she replied.

Theodora turned, ready to investigate.

"Where are you going?"

"I have to find out where that noise is!"

Theo headed for the door. The chanting grew louder as she dashed through the mansion, her ears playing warmer and colder with the strange sound. At last she cornered the sound - it was coming from the playroom!

Theodora approached the door, Starley catching up moments later.

Who is in our house?

Theo signaled her sister to stay back as she crept up to the door and peeked through the keyhole.

To her surprise there were *people* in there. Candles lit the dark room. There was a round table in the center around which four strangers formed a circle holding hands. Two of them looked to be in their 20's, then there was an older man that gave her pause - that *couldn't* be their father?

The most striking figure, though, was an old woman who seemed to be leading the ceremony. She had long, stringy gray hair that fell down her back, she wore a solid black veil and behind it her eyes were solid white.

Theo slowly turned the handle and pushed open the door, which swung open to reveal...nothing? The room was empty.

"What....I don't understand. I just saw them," Theo shouted.

"Who was in here, Theo?"

She ignored her sister's question and began to explore the room. Everything seemed to be in place. Almost everything. One thing was new, a box with the word 'Ouija' across the front of it.

Theo looked at her sister, confirming that neither of them had ever seen it before. She opened the box to find a solid wood board with the alphabet, the words 'Yes,' 'No,' and 'Goodbye' along with some numbers at the bottom. A pentacle and some words in Latin were engraved along the top of the board, but Theo couldn't understand them.

On top of the board lay a strange, heart-shaped piece with a circle at the tip with a glass lens set in it.

All her instinct screams not to look through it, but couldn't help herself. She held the planchette up to her eye and began to inspect the room through the little peephole.

Nothing looked abnormal at first glance, but she continued to glance through the room just in case. It wasn't until she looked over at Star that things began to get... weird. When she looked at her sister she saw a small shadow behind her - a long hand, with fingers as sharp as knives.

Theo's eyes begin to water in fear.

"Starley..." she whispered, hoping the shadow wouldn't hear her. "Come here..."

Starley cocked her head to one side and opened her mouth to speak, but the shadow hand was too quick.

Theo watched helplessly as it grabbed hold of Starley's leg and dragged her from the room in a split second, the door slamming behind her. She could hear Starley screaming and crying, and she sprinted for the door instantly.

Banging on the door to let her out, trying everything to get to her sister. In that moment, Theo found herself face to face with the shadow man, and she screamed as loud as she could, desperate to find an escape. She hit the door - pounding, pulling, and trying anything to get it to budge - but it was stuck fast.

An eerie silence fell, as loud as any thunder. Then she heard it once again - a low throaty crackle. Theo turned slowly, dreading what she would see.

The once-small figure had grown to more than twenty feet tall. It was hunched over, its back and neck brushing the ceiling. It had two normal legs, just as it had before, but now four spider-like limbs protruded from its body, all spread out gripping the walls of the room.

He-*it* wore a top hat, and its face... its face was the stuff of nightmares. Its skin was melted, she could still see it bubbling from unseen flames. Its smile was broken, jagged and raw. The bottom jaw was dislocated from the top and was barely hanging on by shreds of skin.

Theo locked eyes with the entity and let out the loudest and most painful scream of her life.

Starley yanked the door open, as she burst back into the room and she too locked eyes with the creature.

Theo's attention turned to her sister.

"Run!"

The girls ran as fast as their legs would allow, and with each step they could hear the black figure catching up to them.

The thing's twisted, sharpened legs skittered across the walls leaving gouges in the plaster as it moved.

They reached the music room with it right behind them and Theo slammed the door shut. They put their backs against the wood, hoping they could hold it shut with every ounce of strength they had.

Theo looked up, hoping for a miracle, and saw the séance table again. The four strangers were chanting and the old woman was standing over the Ouija board in the middle of the table.

"Hold the door," Theo shouted, heading towards the table.

"Stop! Please stop," she screamed at the old lady.

The old crone didn't react, didn't stop chanting, it was as if she couldn't hear Theo at all.

"They are here," the woman cried out. "Don't break the circle or we will lose the connection!"

"Who are you? Why are you in our home," Theo shouted at the woman, her cries still being ignored.

"Ask your questions, sir," The old woman said to the mystery man.

"Are you girls, okay? Are you safe?" The man asked, his face to the ceiling.

"Stop," Theo shouted again, sobbing even as she recognized her father's voice.

This time it was quiet, but the words seemed to echo into whatever realm the others were in. The older woman turned her attention to the door, she heard a light pounding coming from it as if someone was knocking on the other side.

"D-do not break the circle" the old crone's voice cracked.

Theo put her hand on the old lady's arm and watched as the crone stiffened, her mouth open unnaturally wide as a tendril of black smoke rose from her mouth.

The whole group began to scream and pray - begging for forgiveness for dabbling with dark forces they did not fully understand.

Theo stood still, a jagged but strong connection forming between herself and the old woman, whose eyes went from solid white to the deepest shade of black.

She looked at the man across the table from her and the old woman mimicked her movement.

"Where am I, daddy? I feel so cold" she said, the old woman speaking in sync.

Her father let out a silent sob, his knees buckling.

"You... you died baby," He answered.

"How am I dead? I'm right here daddy... I'm right here!"

The windows burst open with that last shouted word, and everyone shielded their eyes from flying pieces of glass.

The old crone's body fell limply across the table. The room filled with silence as Theo was thrown back into her own reality.

The visions were gone - No séance table, no strangers, and no creature.

I'm... dead?

"There is no way," She turned to her sister but her sister was nowhere to be seen.

"Starley?"

She felt her heart rate spike and ran out in search of her sister.

"Starley," she screamed, running down the great hall. "Starley?!"

She turned a corner and was surprised to see the doctor in the plague mask again. She ran towards him, her hand waving and screaming at him to get his attention.

Nothing worked, he didn't even flinch.

Theo pushed past him, dashing into her mother's room.

But her mother wasn't in the bed.

Both of her parents and her sister were standing at the bedside, obscuring the occupant. Theo slowly crept up next to them, only to freeze at the sigh of *herself* in the bed. She was... *sick*. Her small body was pale and her breathing labored as she coughed up gobs of spittle and blood.

She stood there silently, listening to her family's desperate pleas and prayers. They bargained with any higher power to give their baby girl her health again.

Theo looked away, a chill in her heart, but her gaze was soon drawn back to the bed. She was gone, and now it was her sister, Starley, who lay dying in the bed.

Mother looked distraught - both of the souls she'd brought into this world were being taken from her. Father was trying to comfort her, clearly trying to hold it together for her sake, but he looked just as broken.

Theo watched as Starley's body faded into nothing, and as her parents grew thinner, paler, and more defeated looking. She watched her mother turn and walk from the room and found herself following.

They wandered the silent halls of Morozov Manor for what felt like ages. Her mother alternated between sobbing and begging, pleading for her baby girls to be returned to her.

Theo followed dutifully as Mrs. Morozov headed to the greenhouse. She watched with growing dread as her mother took a long garden hose and tied a noose on the end of it. She followed her mother up the spiral staircase and out onto the concrete ledge where she tied it firmly around one of the gargoyles before slipping it over her head, and she listened as her mother said one last prayer asking for her babies back.

"Mommy," Theo begged. "Please."

Mother must have heard her, because she gave the faintest smile before stepping off into the air.

The hose went taught with an audible crack, but Theo could see that her mother didn't die instantly like you were supposed to when you got hung. Instead she watched her mother twitch and squirm - her face turning purple and her eyes bulging until she finally hung still.

Theo wasn't sure what else to do, so she waited with her mother. She wasn't sure how long it took, but before long she heard her father calling.

The man dropped to his knees when he found Mrs. Morozov, the last bit of light and hope in his eyes fading to darkness.

"Daddy?"

He couldn't hear her, but when he finally stumbled from the greenhouse she followed him. She watched as time passed, and her father became obsessed with increasingly strange and disturbing aspects of the supernatural. She watched as he called a medium he'd seen in the paper, asking her to come down to the manor for a seance - he offered her ten times her normal rate if she could get results, if he could talk to his wife and his girls again.

When they began their first attempt it failed, but he couldn't stop, medium after medium, psychic after psychic came to the house, and all he wanted was a brief second with them, just long enough to tell them he loved them and to make sure that they were okay.

She watched as the events of his last seance unfolded. Had that been the past? Was it the present?

She watched as an ambulance came and took the old woman's body away. Watched as her father sat near-lifeless in his study, an old revolver in his hand, tapping against his temple.

Maybe if he... if this happens, I can rest.

She watched him take a swig of cognac and stand, pressing the barrel of the gun hard against his skull. She didn't want to stay, didn't want to watch, but after all he'd done she felt a sort of obligation.

She flinched when the gun went off. Brains and blood splattered across the room as he dropped in a heap.

Theo waited, but nothing happened.

Surely if her family was gone there was no reason for her to be here any more, couldn't she rest?

If the seance had brought her back, did that mean she was stuck now? And what about-

Her thoughts were interrupted by a low, guttural cracking sound and she spun around to face the door.

She flinched again as something heavy and strong banged against it, the raspy scratching against the wood leaving no doubt in her mind what was on the other side.

She was not alone.

14

Exhibit

By J.W. Wood

Today we are making public extracts from the diary of Professor Luke Oliver. We hope they will explain his disappearance following the discovery of a group of Neanderthals in a remote gully near Mount Hagen, Papua-New Guinea. 31 st March, 2034

Ever since we found the tribe, some of the team think they've made their reputations.

They spend their time drinking beer, eating and laughing at the tribespeople, plotting how they'll write a book or an article about it when they get home.

To them, the Neanderthals are ugly, clumsy and stupid – but to me, these tribespeople have a distinct beauty. Not a physical beauty: a beauty of movement, a slowness and grace we lost in the modern drive towards ever-greater efficiency.

As yet, we've not made any media announcement: the team is banned from saying anything to the outside world. I'm sure it won't be long before word gets out – apparently there's a "strategy meeting" (God!) tomorrow to discuss what we do next.

1 April, 2034 - April Fools' Day.

An appropriate day for some colleagues to make decisions. I've persuaded them our findings will be more compelling if we explain the Neanderthals' way of life.

Naturally, most of these "scientists" want to run straight to the media. All they think about is securing their funding, alongside the usual curse of wanting to be a "celebrity" of some kind.

Take that oaf Bill Holz, our esteemed leader. Professor of Archaeology and Anthropology at the University of Tuscaloosa. Three hundred pounds if he's an ounce, barely able to see over his belly and down into the ravine. A Linen shirt and canvas shorts like Indiana Jones goes to WalMart, endless diet cokes and Pepsi Max. He looks like an ambulatory Christmas pudding, diet sodas notwithstanding.

Holz wants to do a media release, but I've persuaded him to observe the Neanderthals for another week. And by that I mean examining their natural behaviors before word gets out and they're corrupted. Holz, as a "scientist", wants to "experiment" on them to "acquire data." Of of course he does. And since he runs this expedition, all I can do is advise him.

Evening

I walked over to watch the tribe from the lip of the ravine. The sun, a fat bulb sinking into the Western edge of Mount Hagan to our left, the Neanderthal encampment already mostly shadows.

I saw the tribe preparing to sleep. They gathered giant palm leaves together and set them out in circles. Then they laid down on the piles in family groups or singly, none too far from the rest. My eye fell on one couple in particular, their child with its matted orange fur visible from this distance through the gloom. The male and the female slept on either side of the child, keeping it warm and safe. I noticed the mother's tenderness, how the child clung to her, while the father spooned his body around them to offer them warmth and comfort.

Elsewhere, the elders lay awake after the rest of the tribe had gone to bed, keeping watch – or, perhaps, reflecting on the lives they'd lived in this hollow. Then from our camp, the sounds of laughter, drinking and canned music. I sent a quick text to Wendy to wish her and the kids a good morning back in Herefordshire. Then I went to bed, avoiding my colleagues and their mindless partying.

2 April 2034

We carried out the first of Holz's experiments today. His team used a bulldozer to fell two acres of forest and shove the dropped trunks into the ravine. The trees tumbled down, roots and dirt, until they formed a gappy block about fifteen feet high across the ravine's floor. This prevented the Neanderthals from reaching their water supply, a spring tumbling out of the cliff at the far end of the ravine, perhaps half a mile away from where I stood.

I watched the tribe to see how they would respond. At first they were stunned: but within fifteen minutes the practical necessity of how to find water took over. I looked for the Neanderthal couple I'd noticed yesterday. I found them through my binoculars, the mother cradling her child on the palm leaves; the male touching her gently before he left to join the other males and find a way through the fallen tree-trunks. We were supposed to meet with Holz that afternoon to discuss the results of this tasteless "experiment." But I feigned illness and returned to my tent to listen to the BBC.

The news from home goes from bad to worse. Apparently the police surrounded a bunch of climate change counter-protesters in a London alleyway and blocked their exit, then arrested them for affray and breach of the peace. It's a wonder they didn't get arrested for dissent or something. Of course, every protester would have had their online profiles analyzed by the police.

Social media – the modern panopticon, where everything you do and say can be observed and assessed. Why people willingly surrender to that prison is beyond me.

3 April 2034

Today – and not without protest from me – Holz decided to increase the amplitude of his experiments.

First, they undertook a "controlled burning" of the trees they dropped into the ravine yesterday using a flamethrower and cans of diesel. Petrol rained down on the tree trunks, which lit up with thick red flame, a wall of black smoke quilting the ravine until it became hard to see the tribespeople. Pure barbarism, like something out of the Vietnam war.

The Neanderthals panicked and ran to the shallow end of the ravine, away from the fire and their only source of water. They could have climbed out of there: we'd already seen them use vines and outcropping rocks on the more gentle slopes to climb up and forage in the jungle. But in their panic they forgot this option, planted to the spot where the ground rose at the end of their fissure in Mount Hagen's side.

When it became apparent the fire was dying they returned to their camp and addressed the problem of how to get water. As the Neanderthals argued among themselves about how to get through the burning trees, Holz and his team began blasting them with loud rock music from speakers.

The Neanderthals ran amok, trying to climb the vertical stone walls either side of their camp, forgetting that escape was only a couple of hundred yards behind them. Seeing them in distress, I contacted Holz by radio and told him to stop the music and douse the flames. This he did, and by nightfall all was peaceful – though the Neanderthals still appear agitated.

At first, we thought some of the males had gone missing. However, they were out foraging and returned before nightfall to consult with the elders in grunting, rhythmical voices before settling down to sleep on the palm fronds with the rest of the tribe.

4 April 2034 – day off

I'm so disgusted at the way we treat these people I can barely speak to my colleagues. I stayed in my tent all day to avoid seeing anyone, reading an Australian study about the effect of screen time on child development and behaviour. Apparently more than five hours' of screens a day causes patterning in the central cortex similar to that found in patients with early-stage dementia. Yet we persist in encouraging children to use screens everywhere from the classroom to the home, almost as if we sought to create a race of button-pushing morons to be controlled like dogs with simple messages focused on the baser instincts – fear, desire, the rest.

God! I want to be away from here. Not to escape the Neanderthals or the rainforest – quite the reverse. Modernity, in the form of my colleagues and their scheming, is the nightmare I'm trying to escape.

5 April 2034

Holz's latest mad idea is a venture down into the ravine to speak to them. I am opposed for many reasons, mostly anthropological: any undergraduate could tell you what murderous consequences followed after moderns made first contact with the Chagos Islanders a hundred years ago. To this day, there are indigenous Chagos bands who'll kill anyone that gets too close to them. And no wonder.

During the course of my debate with Holz it became apparent he'd received communications from Washington looking for "results." It seems these "results" will justify his request for an increased budget. As scientists, we are both the creators and subjects of a world mired in gross materialism – whatever happened to observation? To consideration? To sensitivity!?

Needless to say, Holz wouldn't listen to my objections. So as far as I'm concerned, I'm getting out on the next transport in three days' time – he can publish, write and appear on TV all he likes. I will not be associated with him, or with this travesty.

Afternoon

I watched Holz's Zeppelinesque form struggle down the soft slopes at the near end of the ravine, accompanied by four researchers and two guides. Through my binoculars, the seven shapes seemed to take forever to get down the slopes half a mile away. During their descent I kept shifting the binoculars to the Neanderthal camp, wondering when they would notice the approaching researchers.

When the Neanderthals spotted our party, their reaction was swift and violent.

As Holz approached within a couple of hundred yards, the males grabbed sticks and stones and hid themselves in foliage either side of the pathway leading from their camp to the slopes at the upper end of the ravine. Some other observer up here must have warned Holz by radio. His team paused, then debated how to escape. As they talked, I saw the Neanderthals shift position, moving out of the foliage, and I shouted at the radio operator to get Holz out.

He repeated my instructions into the radio. Holz's portly form turned and began shambling up the slope followed by the students and guides. The Neanderthals jumped from the bushes and ran towards Holz's party.

The research students and guides, all younger and fitter than Holz, sprinted for their lives leaving Holz struggling his way up through ferns and rocks, the unfamiliar terrain hampering his balloon figure's progress up the slope.

Then the inevitable: Holz got caught.

The rest of his party scrambled up to safety while the males surrounded Holz and pulled him back to their encampment where they beat him senseless. They used sharpened stones to sever his head, bright blood on the stones and mud.

They skewered the head on a tree branch and stuck it in the earth at the edge of their camp. The researchers returned to the cliffs overlooking the ravine a few minutes later – only without our local guides, who'd disappeared into the forest as soon as they'd escaped from the ravine.

Three days until the next transport arrives from Port Moresby, PNG's capital. No question of an airlift – the jungle too thick, the terrain too mountainous.

6 April 2034

Two days left. We have been unable to retrieve Holz's body and his head now perches on that stick two hundred meters below us on the ravine like some rotting fruit from a parallel universe. Yet which world – ours or theirs – is more honest, more real? The head honchos in Washington know about Holz's death. They recommend immediate evacuation. I'm now expedition leader by virtue of seniority, so I put the decision to a vote. A unanimous yes: most of our team couldn't sleep last night. I repeated that the ban on communications via our satellite internet is still in place and more important than ever. I've promised them we will be out of here in 48 hours and that a specialist US Army team will collect Holz's body.

At least the guides who ran away left some weaponry. I order shifts of guards to be set up around our camp, and 24-hour observation on the Neanderthals with binoculars and night-vision equipment. I know we could all be killed – but I cannot get the team out any faster than the day after tomorrow.

Down in the ravine, the Neanderthals look like they're returning to the patterns of behavior we'd first observed: foraging for food, trips up to the spring through the charred tree trunks to fetch water. Again I was struck by their conviviality, the children playing with the palm leaves and fronds they sleep on; the way they slept, worked and rested together. And not a screen or phone in sight. Not even a lightbulb – or a knife, or a wheel. Existence in pure nature. What someone called, centuries ago, a "life brutal, nasty, and short." Now our lives are long, and pleasant – or are they more brutal? The way we sanitize death, "process" our feelings, compartmentalize our emotions.

Our belief that somehow our knowledge is superior to any Man has ever held, and that we will always overcome nature – impossible as that dream is. Man was born to die. When the males leave their encampment to forage outside the ravine, our guards go on high alert. I don't want to cause panic, but I know most of the team were down there when Holz got it, so they'll be nervous. It's my job to make sure we all escape.

7 April 2034

Last night was the most extraordinary I have ever known. I placed guards on watch and retired to my tent armed with a machine pistol, ready for whatever came. Judging by what happened next, I must have been comatose, despite thinking I was awake all night.

At some point I awoke to scratching outside my tent. Assuming it was a monkey or Orang-Utan, I ignored it and buried my head in my sleeping-bag. It soon became apparent the scratching was general around the outside of my tent, so I unzipped first the tent's inner lining, then the outer.

I waited a couple of seconds before opening the flap and shining my phone torch out into the darkness, the other hand on the machine pistol I'd taken to bed with me.

I saw a ring of male Neanderthals surrounding my tent with sticks in their hands. Realizing I was outnumbered, I scrambled out of my tent to face them still holding my weapon, but unwilling to use it.

They formed a square round me like some Roman phalanx. The two either side of me laid hands on me, gripping the flimsy T-shirt I'd worn to bed. They led me from our camp to the lip of the ravine where the slope began its slow descent, littered with rocks and bushes. Then they made me sit facing away from the ravine so that I looked East, looking down away from the ravine into the valley and the lower slopes of Mount Hagen beneath us. Two of them sat either side of me, still sporting the long, sharpened sticks that served them as weapons.

After some time the sun began to rise, its first rays kissing the straggling clouds, then raw sunlight cutting through the smoky air, the edge of its orb rising from the mist. I had never watched a full sunrise before – a pleasure, a spiritual experience that my ambition, my anxiety had wrested from me. When the sun was fully above the horizon, the Neanderthals released me and headed back down the slope towards their village.

I made my way blearily back to our camp, the unused machine pistol limp in my hand.

When I arrived at our camp I found my colleagues slaughtered and the equipment destroyed. I fell down and wept like some character from the Bible, lost and alone by the rivers of Babylon, as the shadows of eight heads skewered on poles lengthened over my filthy, prostrate form.

8 April 2034

As I write this, I may be just two hours away from rescue by the transports or the US military – whichever gets here first. But I no longer wish to be "rescued". If this diary is found, I ask Wendy to remember my love for her and for our children. I ask her to sell our house and car, liquidate our investments, and for her and David and Sally to live as freely as they are able, as far away from civilization as they can.

Do not look for me. Do not hope to hear from me. Just pretend I was never there, I never existed – in the same way as I now wish our so-called civilisation had never been created, and that we all still lived as we were meant to: brief, vicious, rich lives close to Nature and her awful beauty, as true in dealing death as she is in giving life.

Farewell and good luck – you're going to need it.

15

Trauma

By LeAnne Keely

I bet she smells nice.

But I'd find out soon enough.

God I love these late nights. In fact, I might say that staying up all night was my favorite part of all of this if I were ever asked, but I'd be lying.

My favorite part is the blood.

It's so *rich*. So... deliciously *intimate*.

I get so distracted. It really is an awful habit to get into in my hobby.

And speaking of my hobby. Evalyn was finally turning off the light in her second story office. I saw her grab her coat, then disappear into darkness. I tried to contain my excitement, to steady my breathing.

Seventy-one, seventy-two, seventy-three.

Right on cue, she appeared in the glass-wrapped staircase of *KaliKorp*. I don't know what the company does, it never really matters what they do.

Eighty-eight, eighty-nine...

Evalyn paused at the door, and I felt the vein in my forehead throb.

"Ninety-three, she's supposed to turn the handle at ninety-three."

There was no one with me to hear my frustration, but I couldn't contain it. I cracked my neck, counting to ten like my therapist always said to.

It wasn't working.

I fucking hate it when things... when they *deviate*. Everything has a purpose, a *time* and a *purpose*.

I watched her check her pockets, then relax when she found her phone. I was practically foaming at the mouth, didn't she understand she wasn't doing it right? She was going to ruin everything.

One-oh-five, one-oh-six, one-oh-seven...

There it was, she turned the handle and stepped out onto the sidewalk at last.

I checked my watch, it was almost midnight. Poor Evalyn had been working such long hours, she almost never made it home before one thirty.

That was fine, I barely sleep myself. I get it.

Some nights she didn't sleep at all, and we shared a sunrise together. Most of the time she was down by two. As I headed to my car I found myself hoping it would be one of the latter tonight.

It was a quick drive to her house, it *should* have only taken us thirty two minutes and seventeen seconds, but she always took the longer route.

"Such a shame, you *never* take Spring street, always Carmen," I muttered to myself with exasperation. "You could save three whole minutes."

Sure enough, we got caught at the red light. Evalyn was fiddling with her phone while driving, as usual, too busy to even notice the light turning green.

I told myself it didn't matter, hell maybe it was kind of poetic that our last drive home would be just a little longer.

She pulled into her driveway as I continued past, rounding the corner and pulling to a quick stop just out of eyesight. There was, conveniently enough, a streetlight that had been out for months. Just what the hell were my taxes paying for, I often wondered.

Her privacy fence was sturdy, it didn't buckle at all as I climbed it. But that was my Evalyn, always being thorough, making good choices. And I wouldn't have it any other way.

I patted my chest, making sure I had my tools. I knew they were there, I could feel the steel against my skin, but I checked them anyway.

I had a girl ask me once why I kept them inside my shirt, and wasn't I worried I'd cut myself. She didn't get that it was *for her*. I didn't want them to be cold, that might make her uncomfortable. No, better they were body temperature before we got started.

She would spend some time making tea, so I plopped down in the grass and leaned back against the corner of the fence just inside her yard.

Eleven, twelve, thirteen...

"There we are," I sighed with relief. "Back on schedule."

My therapist said the counting was obsessive compulsive disorder, and that I needed some medication.

But I already *have* medication.

She said it might be related to my trauma. *Trauma*. Imagine me, traumatized?

Sixty-six, sixty-seven, sixty-eight.

I'd been counting things more lately, sure. I don't think it had anything to do with Rebecca though.

Rebecca was such a good kid. Her mother and I were good parents too! She fuckin' loved hide-and-seek. They both did, really.

I glanced up, Evalyn was sipping her tea by the sliding glass door. Her breath fogged the glass, I bet it smelled like mint.

No, lemon. She was definitely a lemon kind of girl.

My heart leapt into my throat, was tonight an outside night?

I bit my lip to keep from crying out in excitement as Evalyn slid the door open and took a step out onto the concrete pad of her back patio.

She was so close now, maybe fifty feet.

I caught a whiff of the tea on a warm night breeze.

Mint.

I felt myself scowling, it was supposed to be lemon.

"It's supposed to be lemon, *Evalyn*" I murmured to myself.

I rubbed my temples and shut my eyes, calming myself. I hadn't realized how dry my eyes were, how badly they burned. I must have been staring. See, it's not that I don't blink ever, it's just that I don't blink *often*. I just don't like to miss things, that's all. Perfectly normal.

My therapist has something to say about that as well.

She's got something to say about everything.

She tells me that I have hyper-vigilance, that it isn't unusual for someone who has experienced trauma. *Trauma*. What an idiot.

I opened my eyes, I couldn't risk falling asleep.

Sleep, when had I been able to sleep last?

I thought back, realizing I hadn't slept well since it happened.

I wonder if my therapist would say that was trauma too.

Hide-and-seek was such an irresponsible game to play with children when you were outside. I remembered the number, forty-seven. I hate that number. I wish I could bring myself to skip it, to simply pass it over when I count, but it's so *vitally* important. I have to remember it, I must. How else will I get from forty-six to forty eight?

She stayed outside for six minutes, forty-seven seconds. Of course.

I hate forty-seven.

I hate *squeaking* even more though.

And that goddamn door squeaked when it shut.

I winced, recoiling from the sound. That sound that was so eerily close to tires squealing on asphalt. I covered my ears to keep from hearing the slam of the door into the frame, to keep from reliving the sound of a car hitting two bodies in the street.

The door was shut, and I uncovered my ears at last.

Evalyn really was making this hard for us. She was usually so considerate.

I was restless, so I paced the outside edge of the yard while I waited.

One thousand six hundred sixty-six, one thousand six hundred sixty-seven, one thousand six hundred sixty-eight.

The lights went out and I froze.

I closed my eyes and cocked my head to the side, listening for the soft whoosh of her bedroom window. She loves the fresh air as much as I do.

I must have dozed as I stood there, because I caught myself suddenly falling toward the ground. I stumbled, but kept my footing in the damp grass.

God I missed sleep sometimes. But there was so much to do. I don't like to miss things, totally normal.

I slipped over beneath her window and listened to her breathing. It was easy tonight to pick out her heavy, rhythmic breaths over the soft winds outside. Slowly but surely I heard her drift deeper and deeper.

I imagined that I could hear her heartbeat too, and couldn't help but lick my lips in anticipation. It was with great diligence that I slipped into her room, it would not do to wake her.

A few drops of chloroform on her pillow ensured she wouldn't rise just yet, and I pulled back her covers.

I was pleasantly surprised to see she had a pair of modest shorts and a tank-top on, I didn't want this to be *creepy*. It wasn't supposed to be creepy at all really, I didn't want her to have the wrong impression.

This gave me plenty of room to do my work.

In short order I had her wrists and ankles secured to her bedframe, and I could finally wake her up to get started.

"Evalyn," I whispered, running smelling salts under her nose.

She woke with a start, and immediately tried to scream.

The duct tape over her mouth prevented that, thankfully, but her wide, bright eyes spoke volumes.

I wanted to say something, this part was always so awkward, you know? All I could think about was that thick, bluish vein in her neck. It was pulsing... it was so... so *tantalizing*.

So distracting.

"Shhhh," I reassured her, petting her head gently. "Everything's ok."

She didn't believe me, I could tell.

So frustrating.

"Look, Evalynn," I hardened my tone. "I'm not a bad person, ok?"

She started to cry, I really hate it when they cry.

I couldn't look at her, so instead I turned away and started to lay out my tools.

"There are *so many* types of knives in the world, you know?"

She whimpered, and now I really could hear her pulse if I listened.

After the knives I retrieved a couple of hammers from my bag. One claw, the other a ball peen. Then the only thing I had left was the needle.

"I love this needle," I whispered, as I always do.

I turned to show it to her, but she jerked away as best she could.

"No, see, this is the *exact* needle that they used when I gave a blood transfusion for my daughter Rebecca, it has so much sentimental value to me."

I could tell she wasn't listening, so I grabbed her jaw and turned her face to mine.

"Evalyn this is *important*. You're being *rude*."

Suddenly it hit me, what I'd forgotten.

"No that can't be," I muttered, rummaging in my bag.

But I was forced to admit I had forgotten it.

"Evalyn," I was so embarrassed. "Evalyn I'm so sorry, can I borrow a glass from your kitchen?"

She was confused, but at least she wasn't crying anymore. I took her silence for a yes and helped myself. The cupboard had plenty of options, but I opted for a polished crystal tumbler. It had a certain classiness to it that I thought would really pop.

When I got back to the bedroom I could see that Evalyn was still trying to get loose. Honestly I'm not sure why she wanted to ruin the evening but then, I've been told I have trouble reading others.

"Ok Evalyn I'm sorry, I'm ready now."

I had to start with the hammers, it was important that everything be done just right.

"This is going to hurt very, very badly, ok?"

I think she was trying to ask me why, but I couldn't quite make it out. That's ok though, that's not really an important part I don't think.

The ball peen was fantastic for breaking the ribs. Not all of them mind you, just three, four, and six on the left side. Just like Rebecca.

God, she was crying again. Rebacca hadn't cried. I *know* she didn't cry. I was holding her while the driver called the ambulance! Hell, Ronnie didn't cry either, and she'd had a broken neck!

My wife was so beautiful, her eyes were so wide that day.

That bitch had been driving with her cellphone, so irresponsible. And poor Rebecca, she lost so much blood so *fast*. Not that she had much to begin with.

I remember the glass in her throat, the neat little hole it had made.

I'm not sure how it got onto my lips in the first place, I think I was kissing her cheek while we rode in the ambulance. Must have been sometime before the paramedic pulled me off and shoved the needle in my arm.

That had been my first good look at her, at what that woman had done.

I snapped out of it.

"Now look, I'm being rude aren't I?"

I traded my ball peen for the claw hammer. The tibia, femur, and scapula were much easier with a flatter striking surface. I'd found that out with Terry, but didn't really perfect it until Eliza.

How long ago had that been?

I quirked an eyebrow at Evalyn.

"You know, I don't know the date today."

She wasn't holding my gaze, just whimpering and laying there writhing.

I rolled my eyes as I set the hammer down at last.

"I know, I know it hurts Evalyn. It's supposed to."

At last. The time for blood.

I picked up the needle, checking the long clear tubing for any leaks before I started. It was clean and clear.

Evalyn refused to sit still while I put the needle in her neck, but I managed. Her racing heart saw to it that blood sprang from her body as though it had a will of its own. A line of crimson snaked down the tube, off the bed, and flowed at last into the tumbler I'd placed on the floor.

"Did you know, an average tumbler can fit twelve ounces of liquid?"

She must not have known, judging by the surprise on her face.

I pulled a long, thin filet knife from my assortment and set to work, trying to ignore her screaming.

"Really, Evalyn," I chided her again. "All that noise for what?"

I had to check the cup fairly often, I didn't want to waste anything.

By the time the first glass was ready to drink, I'd nearly finished with her feet, ankles, and calves. My penmanship was improving, I was able to write their names almost fifty times already, and every single one was legible!

I finished the word I was on and then I stood. I retrieved the glass and took a drink, reveling in the creamy texture, the rich, bold flavor. It's hard to describe, a bit like drinking a melted milkshake really. The *weight* of it just seems to hit one differently.

I wiped my upper lip on my sleeve.

"I donated sixty ounces of blood that day, you know."

I took another swig, shuddering a bit in ecstasy.

"Which means you owe me four more of these before we're done."

www.ingramcontent.com/pod-product-compliance
Lightning Source LLC
Chambersburg PA
CBHW060333310726
48976CB00007B/2540